# AU REVOIR, CRAZY EUROPEAN CHICK

## BY JOE SCHREIBER

Houghton Mifflin Harcourt
Boston New York

# To C. Again. Forever.

www.hmhbooks.com

The text of this book is set in Adobe Garamond.

The Library of Congress has cataloged the hardcover edition as follows:
Schreiber, Joe, 1969–
Au revoir, crazy European chick / by Joe Schreiber.
p. cm.
Summary: Perry's parents insist that he take Gobi, their quiet Lithuanian exchange
student, to senior prom, but after an incident at the dance he learns that Gobi is
actually a trained assassin who needs him as a henchman, behind the wheel of his
father's precious Jaguar, on a mission in Manhattan.
[1. Adventure and adventurers—Fiction. 2. Assassins—Fiction. 3. Family life—New York
(State)—New York—Fiction. 4. Foreign study—Fiction. 5. Lithuanians—United States—
Fiction. 6. Coming of age—Fiction. 7. New York (N.Y.)—Fiction.] I. Title.
PZ7.S37913Au 2011
[Fic]—dc22
2011009845

ISBN: 978-0-547-57738-8 hardcover
ISBN: 978-0-547-85632-2 paperback

Manufactured in United States of America
DOC 10 9 8 7 6 5 4 3
4500457668

# Prologue

Describe a significant experience or achievement and the effect that it had on you. (Harvard)

*"You shot me," I said.*

*I was lying on my stomach, wondering if I was going to pass out from the pain. Twenty feet away, she stood with the machine pistol in one hand and the sawed-off shotgun in the other, wiping the blood out of her eyes. It was three a.m. We were in my father's law office on the forty-seventh floor of 855 Third Avenue, or what was left of it. The cops were taking cover behind the couch.*

*She was talking but I couldn't hear anything. The gunfire had left me temporarily deaf.*

*I thought about my father.*

*I took a breath and watched the room wobble at the edges. I was going into shock. The pain wasn't getting any better, and I thought that I would probably black out before I found out how this was going to end. Just as well—I was never particularly good at finishing things.*

*She walked over, knelt down, and wrapped her arms around me. She pressed her lips to my ear, close enough that I could make out the words.*

*"Perry," she said, "I had a very nice time tonight."*

# 1

Explain how your experiences as a teenager significantly differ from those of your friends. Include comparisons. (University of Puget Sound)

Gobi was my mom's idea.

Not that I blamed her. What happened wasn't anybody's fault. I'm not exactly religious, but there is something sort of Catholic about the way guilt gets handed out when blood starts spilling—some for you, some for me, pass it on. Don't forget that guy in the corner—did he get his share?

I guess you could hold Gobi herself responsible, but that's like blaming God for making it rain, or the earthquake in some third world country where half the buildings are still made out of clay. It happened, that's all. Human beings are like the screwed-up children of alcoholic parents in that way, picking up the pieces afterward and trying to make up reasons why. You could argue that's what makes us interesting, and maybe it is to some alien race studying us from a million miles away. From where I sit it just seems pathetic and sad.

Anyway, it all started because my mom's family once hosted a foreign exchange student from Germany back when she was my age. They'd all gotten along famously and Mom still kept in touch with this woman, who was now a family therapist living outside of Berlin. Mom and Dad visited them whenever they went to Europe, and my understanding is that they all had a high old time together, laughing and joking and rehashing the good old days. Just before my senior year of high school Mom thought it would be culturally enriching if our family hosted someone. Dad went along with it in his usual autopilot way—I'm not even sure he was listening to her, to be honest with you.

That's how we got Gobi.

Gobija Zaksauskas.

Mom made me and Annie write her name down twenty times each and we looked up the phonetic pronunciation on a Lithuanian website to make sure we were saying it right. I don't think she would've corrected us anyway. From the moment we picked her up outside the International Terminal at JFK, the most I ever heard her say about it was "Call me Gobi," so we did, and that was all.

Back at the house she got the guest room at the end of the hallway with a private bathroom and her own laptop so she could Skype her family back home. My room was next to hers and at night as I'd sit there memorizing SAT words or banging my head against a college application, I'd hear her voice through the wall, talking in low bursts of consonant-heavy syllables I didn't understand, communicating with family members half a world away.

At least, that's what I thought.

\*       \*       \*

Say "female foreign exchange student" to any group of high school guys and you'll get the exact same look. It's like every single one of the dogs playing poker simultaneously catching wind of the same exotic new Milk-Bone. I'd certainly joked with Chow and the other guys enough about it beforehand, all of us picturing some chic Mediterranean lioness with half-lidded eyes, fully upholstered lips, curves like a European sports car, and legs of a swimsuit model who would tutor me with her feminine wiles before I went off to college.

That's not even funny to me now.

Gobi wasn't much taller than my kid sister, with oily dark hair that she always tucked back in a fat bun behind her head, where it usually escaped to stick stubbornly out, shiny and angular on either side, like flippers on a penguin. Her face all but disappeared behind the massive industrial-grade black horn-rims, their lenses so thick that her eyes looked swimmy and colorless, like two amoebas at the other end of a microscope. She had pasty, instant-mashed-potato skin that could make the smallest single pimple or blemish stand out angrily. Once, and only once, my twelve-year-old sister, Annie, offered her makeup tips, and Gobi's reaction was so awkward that we all pretended that it never happened.

Her one facial expression—a startled combination of hesitation and uneasy befuddlement—might have made her a target for bullying in some high schools, but in the halls of Upper Thayer it made her literally invisible, a shadow always hovering somewhere near the lockers with an armload of books clutched against her chest. Her wardrobe tended toward heavy wool sweaters, smocklike shirts, and dense brown skirts that tumbled down below the knee, avalanching over whatever shape of body might have been hiding under there. The only jewelry she ever wore was a plain silver chain with half a heart dangling from it, halfway down the slope of her chest. In the evenings she sat down to dinner with us, silverware clinking, politely participating in the conversation in her low, formal English, answering Mom's questions about sports or current events until we could all reasonably find an excuse to escape to our separate lives.

One day, six weeks into her visit, she collapsed in the lunch room, passed out in a tray of Salisbury steak and mashed potatoes. I was on the other side of the cafeteria when I heard the screams—Susan Monahan was sure she was dead—and by the time Gobi woke up in the school nurse's office, she'd managed to explain her condition.

"I have spells sometimes," she said. "Is nothing serious." When my parents asked her later why she'd never told us about it, Gobi only shrugged. "Is under control" was all she said.

Except that it wasn't, not really, and from that point she had at least a dozen similar "spells"—they seemed to come in clusters, stress-related—and we were never sure when the next one would come. Eventually we found the technical term was temporal lobe epilepsy—basically a short circuit in the brain's electrical activity, either genetic or brought on by some form of head trauma. Dostoyevsky had it, and Van Gogh, and maybe Saint Paul, too, when he got knocked off his donkey on the road to Damascus, if you believe that sort of thing. All I know is that she wasn't allowed to drive. Once I found her sitting straight up at the dining room table with her eyes half open, staring at nothing. When I touched her shoulder, she didn't even look at me.

In spite of all this, or maybe because of it, I always smiled and said hi to her in the halls. I helped her with her English Lit homework and practically did her PowerPoint presentation on the New York Stock Exchange on the morning that it was due. Even so, whenever she saw me coming, she always looked away, like she knew how much crap people gave me about it—not my real friends; I'm talking about world-class losers like Dean Whittaker and Shep Monroe, rich jerks whose Fortune 500 dads swam the icy seas of international finance looking for their next meal. None of that bothered me. The guys that I hung out with and played music with, the guys in Inchworm and one or two friends who hadn't abandoned me when Dad made me quit the swim team to join the debate team, they seemed to understand, or at least commiserate. *Tough luck, Stormaire, you caught a raw deal there.*

*Yeah, well,* I'd say, *it's not so bad.*

And it wasn't, until my mom asked me to take Gobi to the prom.

# 2

What member of your family has most influenced your identity and aspirations? (Dartmouth)

Prom was two weeks away, and I didn't have tickets. That was my first excuse. Mom said she'd already taken care of that; she had friends on the Steering Committee and there were always a few tickets left over.

I wasn't a prom-type guy; none of us was except Chow, whose girlfriend basically made it clear that they were breaking up if he didn't take her. We ragged him about it pitilessly, of course, but secretly Chow seemed to kind of like the attention. He even made an appointment with a hairstylist in Manhattan beforehand and had the guts to tell us about it. The guy had a masochistic streak—there was no other rational explanation.

When it became clear that the ticket gambit wouldn't work, I played my trump card and reminded my mom that my band, Inchworm, was playing a show that night: not just any show, but our first real gig in New York, at Monty's down on Avenue A. Mom's reaction—"Oh, I didn't realize that"—was enough to make me hope that I might still get off the hook. She'd seen us play locally a few times here and there, but she knew this was different.

Then Dad got involved.

It happened the way it always did, when I least expected it. That's how Dad works. It's probably what makes him such a good litigator, which makes it all the more appropriate that the hour of reckoning happened at his office.

Dad's office was on Third Avenue in midtown, up on the forty-seventh floor, "halfway between God and Broadway," as he liked to say, although that always made me think of someone jumping out a window and screaming all the way down to the sidewalk—*splat.* Twice a week, on Tuesdays and Fridays, I walked straight from school to the train station and caught the New Haven line for the hourlong ride into Grand Central, walked eight blocks north and two blocks over to the offices of Harriet, Statham, and Fripp.

The lobby was huge, with a gigantic fountain and tons of steel and glass. I swiped my personalized magnetic key-card to get in and passed through the turnstile, headed for the bank of elevators on the far side of the security desk. Up on forty-seven, the secretaries usually had a mountain of stuff waiting for me—copying, binding, filing, along with the international satchel that didn't come in until later in the day. As far as part-time jobs went, it paid better than McDonald's, and Dad said that a letter of recommendation from one of the senior partners, maybe even Valerie Statham herself, would ultimately pole-vault me off the waitlist at Columbia, where I was currently stuck, landing me safely into the yes pile. I'd already been accepted at UConn and Trinity, but Columbia was the Grail.

"It's already May," my mom pointed out. "How do we know they haven't already made up their minds?"

"They haven't rejected him yet," Dad said, "all the more reason to get that letter of recommendation. It's not too late."

I was in the copy room up on forty-seven, up to my neck in

Xeroxed depositions, when Dad came in and said, "Your mom tells me you're in the market for a tuxedo."

One thing about the man: you always know when he's sucker-punched you. I put down the stack of pages and turned around to face him directly, just as he'd always taught me to do once I realized I was in for a fight. It was closing in on six o'clock, half the partners were already gone for the day, but Dad's blue eyes shone merrily, his tie was still crisply cinched, and it looked as though he might have just finished shaving. It was a predator/prey relationship straight out of *Animal Planet*.

"I can't do it," I said. "We have a show that night here in the city."

"There will be other shows, Perry."

"Not like this. It took us three months to line up this gig. We're actually paying to play there."

His pupils tightened into rivets, like he had little muscles in his pupils and was actually *flexing* them. "I'd lower my voice if you plan on whining like that. Reputations get ruined for less around here."

"Whose idea was this anyway—Gobi's or Mom's?"

"She's flying home next week," Dad said. "Your mother thinks it would be a good sendoff." He leaned a little closer, and I could smell his cologne, something subtle and expensive. "Look, we all know things didn't turn out exactly the way we'd hoped for her this year. It might be nice to end things on an up-note."

"You still haven't answered my question," I said.

Dad nodded. I understood that I was entitled to such confrontational tactics—it honed the skills for the future Masai warrior of tortious interference that I would no doubt become.

"My understanding," Dad said, "is that Gobi was the one who raised the topic to your mother."

"Wait, you mean she actually *wants* me to take her to the prom?"

10

This was, to say the least, implausible; yet somehow hearing my dad say it out loud with the hum of the copier behind me made it feel true. "She barely even looks at me in the halls, let alone at home."

"But you look at *her*. You smile at her and say hello. You've helped her with her assignments. In a word, you treat her with a modicum of decency and civility, which from what I gather is more than a lot of your classmates can muster up. Who else would she ask to take her?"

I shook my head. "Look, Dad, if it was happening on any other night—"

"But it's not. It's that Saturday night." He waited, but it wasn't the pause of someone anticipating an answer. He was merely allowing his words a chance to sink in. "Your mother will take you out tomorrow to get fitted for the tuxedo. I'm aware that you're making a personal sacrifice, so to sweeten the pot"—I heard the jingle of car keys coming out of his pocket, the stylized Jaguar logo glinting off the copier's green glow as he dangled them in front of me—". . . I'll provide transportation."

I barely looked at the keys. He'd let me drive the Jag only twice in my life, backing it out of the driveway to wash it, and sometimes he let me go out to the garage and sit in it while I studied for my college boards. I already grasped from his tone of voice that this wasn't a negotiating tactic. It was a bone, pure and simple, and he was throwing it because he could. In his mind the deal was done. Whatever happened next was merely lubrication.

"Dad, I don't want to."

"A man has obligations beyond himself, Perry."

"Which means I don't get a choice."

"It *means* in this case you need to put aside your own selfish motives and consider other people for a change."

*For a change:* that was what got me. Looking back, I think I

11

could've gone along with it if he hadn't said that. But he did, and I blew my top. Before I knew it, I snatched the keys off the copier and chucked them across the room, where they bounced off a cabinet and landed on the floor next to several boxes of white bond copy paper.

"*My* selfishness? Everything I do is for other people!" As I said this, I saw my dad's facial expression migrating through surprise, then anger, and arriving at a cool kind of liquid-crystal detachment, all in a matter of seconds, and I realized again, for the hundredth time, how he'd made partner at one of New York's most prestigious firms—the man had the nerves of a test pilot and the internal core temperature of a Komodo dragon. He was the guy you wanted landing the plane when the dials started spinning.

I responded with the only weapon in my arsenal: freaking out.

"You made me quit the swim team to focus on my grades," I said, "and I did it. You made me apply to Columbia and work my ass off for a letter of recommendation. I did it. All *I* have is this band and this show and you need to let me have this, this one thing, just this one thing, okay?"

He waited, enduring me the way you might endure a mediocre street mime, and then in a soft voice: "Are you finished?"

"Yes."

"Good. Your mother will take you out tomorrow for the tuxedo fitting." His hand reemerged from his pocket with a hundred-dollar bill, extending it to me. "I think it would be appropriate if you would offer to take her out to lunch afterward as a gesture of appreciation."

"Keep it," I said. "I have my own money."

"Of course you do," he said, smiling as he walked over to pick up the car keys, and left me standing there.

*     *     *

I went right out to the lobby and hit the button for the elevator. Screw the copies. Let him do it himself.

The elevator went down two floors and stopped again and a tall, elegant woman in a suit got in next to me with a briefcase, talking quietly on a cell phone. She was in her early fifties with brown hair pinned up in a way that showed her slender neck, unwrinkled, the neck of a swan. It took me a few seconds to realize that I was standing next to Valerie Statham, one of the firm's senior partners, the one I was hoping might write that letter to Columbia's admission board. Once, several weeks ago, I'd walked past her corner office and caught a glimpse of Manhattan that existed only for certain individuals occupying a very specific stratum of human achievement. She must have recognized me too, because when she finished her call, she turned and looked me up and down.

"You're Phil Stormaire's son, aren't you?"

"Yeah," I said. "I mean, yes, ma'am." I held out my hand, aware that my face and ears were still burning red from the argument with my father. "Perry."

She shook my hand. "You're clerking here part time?"

"Just helping out. I'm still in high school."

"Graduating this year? What are your plans?"

"Columbia, hopefully. Pre-law."

"Really." She arched an eyebrow. "Have you always wanted to be a lawyer?"

"As far back as I can remember."

"That's good. I always tell people if they haven't wanted it at least that long, they should go do something else." She reached for

13

my hand, then turned it over like a palm reader, examining the cal-luses on my fingertips. "How long have you been playing the guitar, Perry?"

"Ma'am?"

"Your fingers are a dead giveaway. Looks like you've been at it for a while."

I blushed a little for no reason except that she was touching my hand and looking into my eyes, and the realization that I was blushing made me feel even more self-conscious. "Since fifth grade, I guess."

"I dated several guitar players back in college. In fact, I made a career of it. Earned myself quite a little reputation at Oberlin." She smiled and I realized that she was wearing lip-gloss that was almost exactly the same shade as her natural skin tone. "Are you any good?"

"I'm sorry?"

"At the guitar."

"I'm in a band called Inchworm. We're playing a show at Monty's down on Avenue A." Before I could stop myself, I blurted out the rest: "You should come check us out."

"Excuse me?"

"The band," I said. "I could put you on the guest list."

"It's been a long time since I've been down on Avenue A." The elevator dinged, the doors opening on the lobby. "What night is the show?"

"Saturday at ten o'clock. But we usually start a little later than that."

Valerie made a little pout. "That's too bad. I'll be here all night."

"Here at the office?"

"Partners burn the midnight oil, Perry." She winked and gave me a look that I couldn't quite decipher. "Ask your father."

I stepped out and watched her walk across the marble lobby past the fountain, heels clicking toward the door with the measured tick of a stopwatch counting down to silence. As she stepped out onto Third Avenue, I heard a familiar chuckle behind me.

"You can't afford none of *that* fine wine, brother."

I glanced around and saw Rufus, the sixty-eight-year-old security guard, behind the reception desk. He'd been working the six p.m. to six a.m. shift here for forty years, and the building was as much his as it was the firm's.

"Hey," I said, "what'd she mean about my dad?"

"Hey, man, what are you asking me for?" He held up his *Times* in front of his face so that all I could see was the top of his blue cap. "I didn't hear *nothing*."

"Seriously, Rufus."

The paper edged downward, exposing a pair of watchful eyes from behind it. "Seriously? This world's a funny place and it only gets funnier the longer you live in it. And that's the truth." He picked up a Styrofoam cup and held it in my direction. "You want some coffee? Look like you could use a lift."

"No thanks. Anyway, I have to go."

He glanced at his watch. "Little early, ain't it?"

"I'm done already."

"How about an umbrella?"

"There's not a cloud in the sky."

"Suit yourself."

Three blocks from Penn Station, I heard the first rumble of thunder bouncing off the skyscrapers. By the time I got to the station, I was soaked.

# 3

What single word best describes you, and why?
(Princeton)

*"Dick,"* Norrie, my best friend, burst out. "You are being such a *dick!*"

I was up in my bedroom, talking to him on my cell phone, which I had somehow thought would be a better way of breaking the news about going to the prom . . . although now I realized that maybe I shouldn't have waited till the night of the prom to tell him. When I heard how angry Norrie was, I tried to think of how my father would handle this, first by acknowledging his frustrations and validating his emotions as legitimate.

"Look," I said, "I know you're upset, and rightly so."

"Upset? Upset doesn't even b-buh-begin to cover it, you d-dick! You tuh-totally dicked us over, and now you're being a cuh-complete duh-duh-*dick* about it!"

"Okay, but could you maybe find a different word than *dick?*"

"Oooh-kay, m-mister future attorney," Norrie was saying, his stutter getting progressively worse as he became more and more upset. As our drummer, Norrie was one of those people who didn't let himself express anger very often, and witnessing it firsthand was like watching someone go through a particularly dramatic allergic reaction. "Wh-Wh-What are you going to d-d-do about it, h-h-hit me with your *briefcase?* Slam me with a cuh-cuh-class-action s-s-suit?"

"Norrie, calm down."

"Yuh-You t-t-told me you'd t-take c-care of this," he sputtered. "You p-p-promised it wouldn't be a puh-puh-pruh-huh—"

"And it's not a problem," I said, "okay?"

*"Don't finish my sentences for me!"*

"I'm sorry."

"Duh-Does Guh-Guh-Guh . . . ho . . ." I heard him take a breath, forcing himself to relax. "Does Gobi even w-want to go to the p-prom?"

"That's not the point," I said.

That got him started again. "Y-Y-You know what, you're totally *right,* that's *not* the p-p-point, the point is yuh-yuh-you can't ever s-s-sstand up to your duh-*dad,* not even once when it's r-really important."

"Dude," I said, "shut up."

"I d-duh-don't know wh-why you even b-buh-*bother* b-buh-because in s-six y-yuh-*years* y-you're g-guh-going to be j-juh-just l-*like*—"

"Don't say that." Something inside me went cold. "I'm never going to be like him."

"Whuh-whatever you need to t-tell yourself, man." And then, sullenly: "Y-Yuh-You didn't even m-make it to the last p-practice."

"I had to work."

"Exactly."

Enough, I decided. "What time's the sound check?"

"T-Ten o'clock."

"That's plenty of time."

"M-Muh-my ass! What are you guh-going to do, run back to the house, p-puh-push her out of the c-c-car, grab your b-bass, and drive into the city?"

"No," I said. Actually, that had been almost exactly my plan. "I'm going to bring my bass with me."

"Where, in the t-tuh-trunk of the J-Jaguar? You t-told me you were scared to even open it up because you might do something to the latch."

"For your information," I said, "it's a notoriously finicky latch. Have you read *Consumer Reports*? The maintenance on those things is a nightmare."

Norrie snorted. The storm had blown itself out by sheer force of exhaustion, and now he just sounded sad. "You really screwed us on this one, Perry."

"I told you I'd take care of it, okay?" I went over to my bedroom door and clicked it shut, lowering my voice. "Listen. Once Gobi and I get to the prom and she sees what a total error in judgment the whole thing is, there's no way she's going to want to stay. She'll be ready to leave by nine. I'll drop her off, change clothes, and be there in plenty of time. All right?"

Norrie fell absolutely quiet. He and I had been playing music together, writing songs and lyrics, for six years, under a bunch of different names—first we were Tennessee Jedi, then we were Malibu Robot, and then Sasha and Caleb joined and we became the Locker Room Bullies, the Dialups, Skinflip, Barney Rubble, and—for a few miserable weeks—Barn Swallow. I'd agreed to Inchworm because it was the least humiliating name he'd come up with yet.

"You b-better be," he said in a quiet voice. "Seriously, man. There might be p-*people* there tonight. *Industry* people."

"Please," I said.

"Don't you do that," he said. "Don't act like you don't care, Perry, because I know you better. We've b-been friends since fourth grade, man."

"I'll be there," I said, with more confidence than I felt, and clicked him off.


Downstairs, Mom and Dad and Annie were all waiting to make a big deal of my tuxedo. Dad made an even bigger deal about officially presenting me the keys to the Jag, and Mom gave me the box with the corsage that I was supposed to pin on Gobi's dress.

"OMG." Annie covered her mouth and giggled. "You look like a total geek."

"Shut up," I said, "and don't say OMG."

"The G stands for *goodness*. I'm being respectful to God."

"Stop it, Annie," Mom said. "Your brother looks very handsome."

"Mom, come on, admit it: he looks like a colossal dork."

"I remember *my* senior prom," Mom said, and then she actually *did* seem to remember her senior prom and stopped talking.

Something creaked, and I heard Gobi coming down the stairs. She stopped there on the landing and looked at me, and we all stared at her.

My mom was the first one to say anything.

"Oh, Gobi," she said. "You look . . . very nice."

She was still looking at me, and I tried to think of something to say, but the floor had dropped from under my feet and all I could think was *Oh, no.* I turned and locked eyes with my mom. I guess because she'd helped me with the tuxedo, I'd just naturally assumed she would have provided some kind of guidance with Gobi's prom dress.

But it was clear that *nobody* had helped Gobi with her dress.

She wasn't so much wearing the dress as much as lost in it. It was a baggy, shapeless mountain of linen with designs stitched into the fabric, and with a long brown wool skirt, decorated with stripes and cloverleaf, that went down to her ankles so you couldn't even see her shoes. A kerchief covered her head and was knotted underneath her chin. Over her shoulder hung an enormous handmade bag that looked like it was made of some kind of animal hide, replete with pouches and straps and weird little buckles. It was so large that it could have passed for a suitcase, but I had a feeling it was supposed to be her purse.

"Is a traditional Lithuanian ceremonial costume," she said, her voice all alone in the silence. There was a thumbprint over the left lens of her glasses, right in front of her eye. "Was my mother's."

"Well, it's lovely," Mom said.

"Thank you, Mrs. Stormaire."

"Perry?" Mom held out the corsage for me, and I went over and unlatched the pin, trying to find a spot to plant it. I'd never been this close to her before, and I could smell her, the scent of unfamiliar soap and detergent in the fabric of the clothes. My hands trembled a little bit, and I stabbed myself with the pin.

"Ow!" I pulled back my hand, watched the dot of blood ooze from my fingertip. "Shit!"

*"Perry!"*

"Sorry, Mom. It's just the stupid pin—"

"Are you bleeding?" Gobi asked.

"Well, don't get any on your shirt!" Mom said.

I sucked my finger. "I'm fine, it's nothing."

"You should not be afraid of a little blood," Gobi said. "Life is full of it."

I glanced up at her, wondering if that was supposed to be a joke, but her face was unreadable as ever—even her expressions seemed to require subtitles. Annie started laughing and Mom got me a Band-Aid. Dad stood there watching me the whole time with that whole ah-the-human-comedy-ain't-it-fascinating look on his face as Gobi and I walked out to the Jaguar.

It wasn't quite twilight, but the air had already turned chilly. I went around and opened the passenger door for her, then walked back and got behind the wheel, feeling, in spite of everything, a kind of automotive stagefright. As I turned the key and felt the Jag's engine throb to life under the hood, I saw Dad standing in the doorway, one hand raised in silent salute, except then I saw it was a clenched fist and it looked more like a gesture of victory. Anger bubbled up in my stomach, and I gunned the engine a little, feeding it gas until it made me feel better, like I knew it would. Then we slipped down the driveway and into the cool promise of night.

# 4

Tell us about the most stimulating conversation
you've had. (University of Michigan)

It was silent as we drove to the school. I turned on the radio, couldn't find anything worth listening to, and switched it off again.

"You are embarrassed of me," Gobi said.

I looked over at her with the great sloping heap of the bag on her lap. It lay there like a big dog that had gone to sleep. "No, I'm not," I said. "Not at all."

"It is all right for you to say. I can see it in your eyes."

"That's not true."

She stared straight ahead. "Next week I will fly home."

"Right." I didn't dare ask about her experience here. "You must, uh, really be looking forward to seeing your family again."

She didn't say anything. The atmosphere dropped a degree or two, seeming to thicken invisibly around us, as if someone had run a length of garden hose through the back window and was slowly filling the Jaguar with a lethal dose of carbon monoxide. I practiced holding my breath, just in case.

"I just want to tell you," she said, "I appreciate what you are doing for me. Thank you."

"Don't worry about it." Something in me snapped, and I was talking again before I knew it. "Can I ask you something, though?"

She turned to face me, patiently.

"What made you really want to go to the prom with me? I mean . . . I'm fine with it, but—"

"But clearly you are *not* fine with it, Perry."

"What?"

"You had no wish to bring me to this prom. I know this. You do not think I can see these things for myself?"

"Well, my band is playing a show tonight in New York," I said. "It's kind of important."

"Even if they were not," Gobi said, "you would still not want to take me to the prom, yes?"

"No. I mean, yes. It's just that I was surprised. It didn't seem like anything you'd really be interested in, that's all."

She didn't reply, just kept both hands wrapped tight around the handle of her bag and looked straight ahead as we drove up into the school parking lot. Just before we got out, she turned to me again.

"You do not know me, Perry."

"No, I guess not."

"Perhaps by the end of the evening you will."

I looked at her. What was that supposed to mean? Ever since her comment about blood, I realized I'd been thinking about Sissy Spacek in *Carrie,* the high school loser in her homemade prom dress, drenched in pig blood, unleashing a firestorm of psychokinetic destruction on the high school gym. Ever since I'd seen that movie on TV when I was eight, I'd been queasy at the sight of blood, especially mine. Probably most proms didn't turn out that way, but what if this one did?

The distress must have shown on my face, because for the first time ever, Gobi actually laughed. Her eyes sparkled, a bright and glinting green behind her glasses, and for an instant the light transformed her entire face—the bland, expressionless mask slipped away to reveal an actual *girl* underneath: feminine, uninhibited, spontaneous, and alive. It occurred to me that I might have been missing something this whole time.

"You handle this car very well, Perry."

"Yeah, well, it's a pleasure to drive."

I parked and got out, walked around the car, offering my hand, and she slipped out of the leather interior. She felt lighter somehow, despite her heavy, rustling outfit, gliding almost gracefully alongside me toward the entrance. I could already hear the music inside, the murmur of people, kids I'd gone to school with for the last twelve years, dressed up and pretending to be the adults we'd all eventually turn into, whether we wanted to or not.

*Maybe it'll be okay,* I thought.

I held the door for her, and we stepped inside.

**5**

Sartre said "Hell is other people," while Strei-
sand sang "People who need people are the lucki-
est people in the world." With whom do you agree?
(Amherst)

I don't know what I'd been hoping for, but right away I knew that coming had been a big mistake.

I couldn't remember the theme of the prom but it seemed to be something along the lines of Social Darwinism Under the Stars. Lights and shimmering tinsel had transformed the gymnasium into a pulsating soup of glandular hostility. Nobody actually said anything, not at first, but I could feel dozens of eyes on Gobi as she stepped through the door, and I saw the expressions on the faces of the girls and the guys—disbelief, amusement, that vicious dinner-is-served delight—as they stared at what she was wearing. She wasn't invisible anymore. She'd stepped dead-bang into the spotlight, and she'd painted a big bull's-eye on her head. I thought about those South American cattle farmers who shoved the weakest, scrawniest cow in the river upstream, protecting the rest of the herd while schools of piranha ripped the poor sacrificial heifer to shreds. Whether or not that actually happened, I didn't know or particularly care—as a social model for high school dynamics, it was too cruelly perfect.

On stage, a band that nobody had ever heard of was in the middle of massacring a Radiohead song, but the noise still didn't seem to drown out the whispers around us.

"You want some punch?" I asked.

"Yes, please."

I made my way across the room to the tables set up on the other side. Chow was there with his girlfriend, and he gave me this incredulous look as if he'd somehow never actually expected me to go through with tonight's events. Ignoring him, I scooped up two plastic champagne flutes of punch and brought them back to Gobi, who was standing alone at the edge of the dance floor with a ten-foot radius of open space surrounding her, and handed her a glass.

"Thank you."

"Sure." I gulped my drink, found a place to put my glass, and struggled to keep my hands from running through my hair. Gobi watched the band play. It was impossible to tell what was going through her mind, but she seemed more weirdly *here,* alive and in her element, than she'd ever been while trudging the halls of Upper Thayer with her books under her arms, or sitting at our dining room table.

Finishing her punch, she turned to me and looked up.

"Would you like to dance?"

"I really don't—"

Her hand found mine, fingers slipping between mine with surprising firmness. "Dance with me, Perry."

I had no idea how it was going to go, but it wasn't awful—we got lost in a sea of shuffling couples, held stiffly on to each other, keeping six careful inches of open air between our bodies. It was just dancing, that was all. Slow circles. Zero eye contact. Gobi's blouse crinkled stiff and unyielding in my hands, like armor made of hotel curtains, and when the third song ended I glanced at my watch and saw that it was somehow past eight already.

I was about to say something when a dump-truck load of bricks smashed into my shoulder, knocking me sideways toward Gobi. She dodged out of the way, surprisingly fast, and I found myself flailing toward the floor, hearing a burst of cold laughter behind me.

"Hey, Stormaire, nice of you to bring your cleaning lady to the prom."

Turning around, I saw Dean Whittaker standing there, hands in his pockets, grinning. Lanky, curly-haired, gifted with the rubbery face of a natural clown, Whittaker wore what was no doubt a tailored Armani tuxedo, with Shep Monroe pasted to his right shoulder like some hideous life-size ventriloquist dummy. I didn't even know what they were doing in a public school. Whittaker and Monroe were as wealthy as they were psychotic, and looking at them, you got the feeling that the prom was nothing more than a sadistic giggle between big over-oxygenated whoops of special rich person air that they had flown in exclusively from Switzerland. The girls they'd brought to the prom didn't even go to Upper Thayer; they were daughters of their parents' friends, families whose money and influence flooded endlessly from some completely different sphere. They both looked almost transcendently bored.

"Back off," I said, already aware of how lame it sounded.

"Back off?" Whittaker's grin widened, showing perfect teeth. "Why should I? Is it gonna *get ugly?* Are you going to *bring the pain?*" Hands still in his pockets, he waded a step closer. "Tell you what, douche stool, I'll do whatever you say on one condition: you let me videotape you and your date when you start going at it later tonight." His eyes flicked over to her. "I want to see you even try to find an actual girl underneath all that body hair."

"That's it," I said, and came forward, swinging at him. I hadn't been in a fight since sixth grade, and Whittaker must have seen my fist coming from a mile away, because he was already dodging and springing up at me, tagging the side of my chest with a tight, hard right that stung like a golf ball. I went over sideways, counting my ribs. Somewhere off in the distance, behind rippling acres of pain, I heard Shep Monroe yodeling out a moronic laugh.

"You're a ballsy little prick, Stormaire." Whittaker had my face squashed in his hands while spitting right into my ear. "You've got a real set of oysters on you, messing up my prom with that piece of Euro-trash."

"Don't call her—"

He shoved me backwards with a snap of the arms, pistoning me hard enough that I half expected to wake up in an ambulance. People were staring, but when I glanced around again, he and Monroe and their two vacant-looking society dates had vaporized into the background.

I caught a glimpse of Gobi looking back at me from where she'd seen the whole thing, her expression as unreadable as ever.

"Hey," I said. "You want to get out of here?"

She nodded. "You should bring the car around." Her eyes flicked off in the direction of the ladies' room. "I need to fix my makeup."

I realized she probably just wanted a chance to compose herself. Maybe she just wanted to slip away completely. After what just happened, I couldn't blame her.

Hell, maybe I'd get lucky and we could end this whole thing now.

*   *   *

She came out ten minutes later and got in the car without a word.

"Look," I said, as we drove away, "I'm sorry about that."

"You should really learn how to fight."

I turned to her. "What?"

"You telegraphed your punch. That boy got lucky. You should have broken his nose."

"I didn't realize you were such an expert on the pugilistic arts," I said. "Maybe you can give me some pointers."

Gobi shrugged. "If you like."

"I guess you heard what he said about you."

"Tch." She wrinkled her nose. "The opinion of such a *subinlaizys* means nothing to me."

"What's that mean?"

"It is what you would call . . ." She hesitated, trying to come up with the proper translation. "What is it that dogs do?"

"Chase cars?"

"No." She shook her head. "Lick their own balls."

"You called him a . . . ball-licker?"

"What," she said, "you are scandalized?"

"No," I said, "I just didn't know you knew words like that."

"Are you joking with me? My language is rich with curses."

"Like what else?"

"Well, you could call him . . . *Gaidzio pautai*—that means chicken balls."

"*Chicken* balls?"

"If it were me, though," she said, "I would simply crush his windpipe so he could say no more offensive things to women."

29

"That's what you would do to him, huh?"

"For a start, yes."

"You're full of surprises, you know that?"

"I told you that you would know me better by the end of the night."

"I dunno," I said, "I mean, you've been here nine months. How come you never acted like this before?"

She didn't answer. After a second I looked at the clock on the dashboard. It was almost eight thirty now. I realized that I had to take her home, but given what had happened, I didn't think I could just swing by the house and order her to get out.

"You, ah, want to go anywhere else while we're out?"

"I would like to go to the city."

"What?"

She pointed at the sign up ahead that read NEW YORK CITY —48 MILES.

"You want to go to New York?"

"This is my last week in United States, Perry. You can show me around, yes?"

"We were just there last week, remember?"

"I am not talking about a Broadway show with your parents and your little sister. I am talking about Manhattan at night with you. Do you understand the difference?"

"Are you serious?"

"Do I look like I am joking?"

I felt myself starting to nod. This could actually work in my favor—if Gobi really wanted to go into the city tonight, then I'd be clear to play the gig at Monty's, and even my dad couldn't say anything about it. "Okay," I said, "I mean, if that's really you want." We were back in town now, our little village square, and I hit my turn signal and started edging toward the left lane. "But I need to go home first and switch vehicles—"

"No." She grabbed the steering wheel. "We take this car."

"Wait, what are you doing?"

"The Jaguar—it is a nice car, yes? Is fast, yes?"

"Yeah," I said, "it's fast, but—"

"So we take it."

"No."

"I thought you said it was a pleasure to drive."

"To the prom, yes. To New York City, not so much."

She clicked her tongue and stared at me. *"Sliundra."*

"What's that mean?"

"It means . . . how do you say . . . ?" Gobi nodded at herself, down there. "Pussy?"

*"Pussy?* You're calling me a pussy?"

She nodded.

"Okay, Gobi, let me explain something to you. This is, like, an eighty-thousand-dollar car, which my father loves like a child—I'm not taking it into Manhattan, and that's final."

"You always do what your father says?"

"When it comes to the car, yeah."

She was smiling at me again, the way she had when we'd first arrived at the prom, but now more challenging, not quite playful. "I see you, the way he talks to you. He runs your life." Her voice dropped into a cruelly accurate imitation of my dad's stentorian tone. *"Perry, you need to work harder. This is not acceptable. You will never get into Columbia with grades like these. How will you succeed in life?"*

I felt my internal temperature rise past my lips, cheeks, and forehead. "That's not true."

"He tells you to do something, you do it. You spend your whole

31

life afraid you will somehow disappoint him. And that is no way to live."

"Look," I said, "I'm sorry, but you don't know me that well. I mean, maybe you've lived in our house for a while, but you don't know anything about how it really is with us."

"Prove it."

"What?"

"You heard me. What are you being so afraid of?"

"That's not the point. I'm not doing this. Understand?"

She sighed. "Your father said that you could drive the car, yes?"

"Yes, but—"

"He did not say *where* you could drive it."

I glanced down at the keychain dangling from the ignition and thought about my father handing it to me at his office, one more chain that he held one end of while offering me the other. I put my foot down on the accelerator. The throb of the V-12 engine rippled through me in one solid wave.

"Just for a quick trip."

Gobi nodded as if she'd expected nothing less. She reached into her enormous bulky handbag and pulled out a BlackBerry. Had I ever seen her use one before? Her fingers swept quickly over the keys, tapping something in and holding it up so I could see.

"I want to go here."

I looked. "What, the 40/40 Club? Are you serious?"

"You are familiar with it?"

"Well, yeah, it's Jay-Z's club, but—"

"Good," she said, and took the BlackBerry back, tucking it away. "Then get us there."

"Why there?"

She shrugged. "I read about it in a magazine. I want to go there."

"I doubt they'll let us in."

"Why are you always so seeing the dark side of things?"

"That's kind of how I am when it comes to stuff that's totally impossible," I said. "Other than that, I'm a regular Mr. Sunshine."

She laughed.

"What?"

"You are funny."

"I'm glad you think so. This might be as interesting as the night gets."

"I doubt that very much," she said.

I downshifted and focused on my driving. It felt good to be bad; I was starting to get used to the idea. "So, 40/40," I said. "You just read about it in some magazine and decided that's where you wanted to go?"

No answer from Gobi. I glanced back at her. Her head was resting against the window, tilted so that I couldn't see her face.

"Gobi?"

Still no reply. I reached for her shoulder and squeezed slightly, then harder. She made a groaning croak in the back of her throat, adjusted her shoulders, then sat up and blinked at me with a disoriented expression, realization seeping into her eyes.

"Oh," she said.

"You all right?"

She nodded.

"You had a seizure?"

No answer.

"Listen . . . maybe we should just go home."

"No." A single, brittle syllable. "It has already passed."

"Are you sure? Sometimes when you have those . . ."

"I am *fine*, Perry." She nodded out the windshield. "You just drive the car."

# 6

Discuss how your travel experiences have affected you as a student and a citizen of the world. (University of Florida)

Forty-five minutes later we were in the Flatiron District, looking up Twenty-Fifth Street at a row of stretch Expeditions parked outside the towering, two-level club where people lined up inside the red velvet ropes waiting to get in. I'd seen it in magazines, but this was as close as I'd ever been in person.

"They're never going to let us through the door."

"Do not always think—"

"—on the dark side of things, right, I get it."

Gobi gathered her bag, opened her door, and ducked out. "Meet me inside."

"What if—"

She was already gone. I sat there for a moment, looking through the windshield at the lights of downtown while taxis rolled up behind me, blasting their horns. The valet appeared next to my window, a slick ghost.

"May I help you, sir?"

"Park it somewhere safe, please," I said, taking the ticket and climbing out, aware of my rented prom tuxedo like I'd never been before. Nobody else seemed to notice except the bouncer, who flashed me an indifferent look and gestured me forward. He was probably going to tell me there was no way a kid in a rented tuxedo was going to be seen outside this kind of club. I pretended not to notice, keeping my eyes peeled for Gobi and wondering when we could get out of here.

*"Hey!"* the bouncer shouted, waving me up until I couldn't ignore him anymore. People were staring. Blushing, getting ready to be yelled at, I went toward him, and he opened the rope to let me through. "She's in there."

"Excuse me?"

"Your date."

"Oh. Thanks."

"Whoa." His hand fell on my shoulder. "You have ID?"

"Yeah, I . . ." After digging out my wallet, I fumbled for my license and then waited while he inspected the birth date. He stamped my hand with a big red stamp: UNDERAGE.

"No alcohol. And you can't sit at the bar."

"Okay."

I stepped inside.


Everything was different in here: sounds, smells, lights, music. People who seemed to belong to some exclusive group—adults, sophisticates, citizens of the world—were packed up tight against the bar. I passed underneath a storm of silent images from the sixty-inch plasma screens playing ESPN from the walls. Up ahead, white swing chairs with yolk-yellow interiors dangled from the ceiling, looking like giant hard-boiled eggs, while the most beautiful women I'd ever seen sat inside them swinging their legs and sipping drinks from champagne glasses. Men in suits, tall guys in sunglasses who looked like NBA players, more gorgeous women, singles, hipsters, all lingered around the marble floors and the staircases. After a moment of standing there, I saw Gobi at one of the tables near the back and went over, trying to make sense of her presence here.

"How'd you get us in?"

"Sit down." She pushed a tall glass in my direction without actually seeming to look at me. "I ordered you a Pepsi."

"Thanks."

"I will be right back."

"Gobi, wait a second—"

She was already gone again, angling into the bathroom. I sipped my Pepsi and tried to look as if I were drinking Courvoisier. I didn't know how she'd gotten us in or what we were going to do next, but that feeling of sensory detachment was coming back, making everything feel both too real and not real at all. It was after nine thirty—closer to ten now—but I figured if I paid for my ten-dollar Pepsi and got out of here quickly I could still make it to sound check downtown. As long as nothing stupid happened in the meantime.

Gobi had been gone for what felt like ages. I pulled out my phone and checked the time. Three Wall Street–looking jocks at the door were eyeing me as if they were about to come over and ask if they could have this table. Glancing back in the direction of the women's bathroom, I saw a slender young woman in a little black dress and wraparound sunglasses sauntering directly toward me, arms swinging slightly, hips snapping back and forth like a metronome beneath the stretchy fabric. Her red lipstick seemed to cut through the air. She dropped her bag onto the table next to my drink with a thump.

"I changed my mind," she said. "I want to go."

I stared at her. *"Gobi?"*

"Have them bring the car around."

I was still staring at her, my brain trying to swallow what my eyes had already bitten off. It was Gobi—except it *wasn't*. Gone was the muddled look, the poached and blemished skin, the oily split ends. Everything was focused, clean, and smooth. She'd unleashed her hair, which now tumbled down in easy, effortless, chocolate-colored tumbles and quotation marks around her shoulders and face. The tight, lithe body that she had been hiding under forty-two pounds of eastern European wool was right here in front of me now, stretching the dress in all the right places. I could almost hear the seams creak as she breathed. The only similarity to the girl who had gone into the bathroom was the half-heart pendant that still dangled around her neck.

"What happened to you?"

She lowered the sunglasses, showing me eyes so green, they stung like peroxide. "You are staring."

"Sorry, but *yeah*."

"I will pay for the drink. Meet me outside." She picked up her bag and glanced over to the front of the club, where several guys in bridge-and-tunnel suits and greasy-looking haircuts were lingering over drinks with girls in barely-there dresses. "Not in front of the window."

I stood up, looking back, almost walking into a table as I watched her cross the room. Outside, I handed the valet my ticket. When he brought the Jag around, Gobi still hadn't come out. I got behind the wheel and nosed up as close to the front of the club as I dared, then pulled out my cell phone and dialed the one person who would most appreciate this, meaning the one guy I was pretty sure would believe me.

It rang three times.

"Yo, Perry?" I could hear the noise and music of the prom in the background.

"Chow."

"What's up, dog? That's whack about what happened at the prom with Whittaker and—"

"Chow, listen. I'm in the city."

"What, what? The ci-*tay?* That's cool."

"No, listen. We're at the 40/40 Club—"

"Fawty-Fawty," Chow said, not exactly hiding that he was an eighteen-year-old Korean kid who spent too much time listening to Young Money and playing World of Warcraft. "Heard *that,* yo. You the man, Perry. You *more* than the man. You the—"

"Chow, will you shut up a second and listen?" I said. "I'm here with Gobi. She just came out of the bathroom, and she's, like, completely transformed into this total epitome of hotness."

"Hold up," Chow said, dropping the hip-hop affection entirely. "We are talking about the same foreign exchange student here? The one that kicked those guys' asses at the prom?"

"Wait," I said, "what?"

"You didn't hear about that? Shep and Dean? That's what I was going to tell you. After Whittaker punched you, she came back and finished it. She put them both in the ER, dude. Ambulance ride on prom night. Where were *you?*"

"I was . . ." I started, and stopped. I was remembering her telling me that she had to go fix her makeup. Asking me to bring the car around while she—

Suddenly the front window of the club shattered, spraying glass into the street, and something came flying out, the body of a greasy-haired man in a gray suit bouncing across the hood of the Jaguar so that his bloody face pressed against the windshield in front of me, ten inches away. It looked like a flesh-colored candle melting against the glass, eyes open, glazed and lifeless.

I jerked back, screaming, dropped the phone and started fighting to get out of the car when Gobi appeared next to me, gliding down into the passenger seat and yanking me back in.

"I told you not to park in front of the window," she said.

# 7

Reflect on your reaction to a crisis or a critical moment in your life when thinking as usual was no longer possible. Describe the event and tell us how it changed your thought processes. (Ramapo College)

Here's me: still screaming.

"There's a dead guy on the car! Oh, man. What the hell? *There's a dead guy on top of my dad's car!*"

Out of the darkness, something pinched my shoulder, hard enough to cut through the fog of panic. Gobi was squeezing me just above the socket of my arm, and when I looked over, the sunglasses were off and her eyes were drilling straight into mine.

"You should put the car in reverse, Perry. That will get the body off your car."

My gaze went down to the bulky bag between her knees, the only remnant of the person she'd been fifteen minutes earlier. The bag was open and I could see a gun resting on top of a bundle of clothes, next to the BlackBerry.

"*You* did that? You shot that guy?"

"Back up the car, Perry." Her voice was totally calm. "Before the police arrive."

I was still grappling with the latch to get the door open, fighting to get out of the car, when Gobi swung one boot-clad leg over the gearshift and stepped on the gas while simultaneously dropping the Jag into reverse. We jolted backwards hard enough that I felt my incisors click together and the dead man's body flopped forward and disappeared completely from the Jag's hood. Gobi whipped the wheel hard so that we swerved around between a stretch Hummer and Lexus waiting for the valet.

"Now," she said, "drive."

I shook my head, thrashing like a fish in a net. "Let me out! You can have the car! Just let me out!" Where was the door handle? I'd only had to get out of the Jag's driver's seat three or four times in my entire life, counting the times that I'd worked up the courage to sneak out to the garage and sit in it, and my fingers were still raking the interior trying to locate the handle when I felt something hard and hot press against my right temple. I could smell heated steel and gunpowder very close by.

"Do you remember when you helped me with that PowerPoint presentation for Mr. Wibberly's economics class?" Gobi said. "You were thinking very clearly then, Perry. You are not thinking clearly now." Her voice became an odd combination of gentle and didactic, as if she were explaining something completely simple to a complete simpleton. "I cannot drive a car. You know this."

"It's New York City! Who needs a car?"

She touched my hand. "I need you."

I looked right and left. Outside the club, people were gathering around the broken window, staring at the body sprawled out on the street, the body that had seconds earlier been on the hood of the car.

Some of them were glancing back toward us. I could feel the presence of the gun hovering just outside my peripheral vision like some suicidal thought that I was too terrified to acknowledge. "Who are you? You're a foreign exchange student! You're in high school!"

"I am twenty-four years old."

*"What?"*

"Drive the car." The barrel of the gun pressed harder on my skull. "I will not ask again."

I shifted the Jag into drive and pulled out into the street, every part of my body shaking at different vibrational frequencies. Gobi reached over and hit the windshield wipers, smearing the dead man's blood across the glass in a gruesome double rainbow. She squirted wiper fluid and ran them again. The glass got a little cleaner. Now I could see the lights of Broadway up ahead, shining away in drizzled bloody streaks. In the rearview mirror, the crowd in front of 40/40 was getting bigger by the second. Sirens were rising up in the distance.

"I can't believe this. This isn't happening."

"You can drive a little faster."

"I am!"

"You are driving five miles an hour."

Up ahead, the light was turning red. "Please, okay, just . . . put the gun down, okay?"

"Here." She lowered it until the barrel was resting against my side. "Do you prefer this?"

"You shot him. You totally just shot that guy back there. I think I'm gonna throw up."

She didn't say anything.

"Who was he?"

"No one."

*"What?"*

"Keep going. Get in the right lane. We have to go downtown."
With the gun still pointed at me, she reached into her purse and
brought out the BlackBerry, tapping keys. "Take a right and get on
Broadway."

The intersection was crammed with pedestrians and cabs, and
two NYPD cruisers parked at the light. We were still close enough to
the club that I could see the crowd getting bigger outside, and cops
were getting out, fighting their way through traffic. "We're screwed.
We're so utterly, hopelessly screwed."

"Just get us away from here and I will explain everything."

"That's a red light!"

"Run it."

"I can't! I'll hit somebody!"

I ran the red light. Behind me, blue and red lights started swirling. Not even thinking, I slammed on the brakes. My heart stopped
and everything below my waistline just seemed to disappear—a total eclipse of the balls. I saw two cops get out and start walking up
toward the Jaguar on either side. To my right, Gobi reached into her
bag and draped a kerchief over the gun she had jammed against my
side, pushing it tighter into place.

"If you say anything wrong, I will kill you first."

The cop bent down to my window, glaring straight at me.

"Get out of the car," the cop said.

# 8

Using actual details, create a completely fictional
version of some pivotal moment in your life.
(Oberlin College)

For a second I didn't react. Muscles locked on to tendons; ligaments grabbed hold of bones. It wasn't that I didn't *want* to move; my body just wasn't about to obey, almost as if it thought that if it didn't budge, it could somehow negate that all of this was really happening. Police lights splashed across the Jag's interior, filling it like rising water crackling with lethal electric current.

"Did you hear what I said?" the cop said. "Get out."

"I . . ." I felt the barrel of Gobi's gun gouging my pelvis. "I can't."

The cop gazed at me with depthless indifference. He looked like the kind of guy that would rather be smashing some crack dealer's face against the pavement or tossing a pedophile off a fire escape but was willing to use me as a little warm-up on a slow Saturday night.

"I can't get out," I said. "My legs won't move."

"What, you're handicapped?" He whipped out a flashlight and

shone it down at my feet, one of them hovering over the gas, the other resting above the clutch. "You think that's funny? My brother lost a leg in Fallujah—you think *that's* funny?"

"No, of course not. I'm sorry."

He flipped the bow tie around my neck. "Where did you come from tonight?"

"We were at the prom," Gobi said from beside me.

"The prom?" His tone of voice hadn't changed. "License and registration, now."

I dug for my wallet, handed him my license, and reached for the glove compartment for the registration.

"Wait a second." The flashlight froze on the windshield. "Is that blood?"

"That? Oh, yeah," I said. "I hit a deer."

"You hit a deer."

"Yeah . . ."

"Where, Madison Square Garden?"

"The Connecticut Turnpike," I said. "It ran out in front of the car."

He looked disgusted. "Get out of the car."

What happened next couldn't have taken more than a second or two, but in my mind it lasted forever. I saw the cop's hand reach through the open window and realized that he was going to drag me out of the car if I didn't comply. Except that Gobi was going to shoot me first. I would die on the sidewalk at the corner of Twenty-Fifth and Broadway with a bullet in my lung, having spent just enough time inside the 40/40 Club to take one sip of Pepsi. My headstone would read PERRY STORMAIRE: HE DIED A VIRGIN.

Then—

The explosion shattered the air somewhere behind me, a deafening blast that sent the cop ducking for cover. I caught a glimpse of flame in the side-view mirror and saw the exterior of the 40/40 Club plume outward onto the sidewalk in a churning horizontal cloud of smoke and dust. People scurried like rats out into the street, and cars swerved and slammed on their brakes to dodge them. When I looked up again, the cop was running back to his car, shouting something to his partner. Car alarms were yelping up and down Broadway in all directions, the noise rising up through the debris.

"What the hell was that?" I shouted.

Gobi tugged my arm. "The light is green. Go."

Cranking the wheel, I swung out onto Broadway, weaving my way downtown, hardly aware of what I was doing. I kept looking back until I couldn't see the club anymore.

"What happened back there?"

"Semtex. I left it in the alley outside the club."

"What? You did that too?"

"No one was hurt. Just a distraction."

"Just a distraction? That was a bomb!"

"Only a little one."

"Only—" I blasted through a red light, yellow cabs hitting their brakes, blaring their horns and missing our back bumper by centimeters. "I can't believe this."

"Watch the traffic." She was working the BlackBerry again. "We need to get to West Street, Battery Park. Stay on Broadway. It should only take ten minutes."

The delayed shock was hitting me now, the combined effect of everything that had just happened collapsing over me in a blinding, numbing wave. Studying for the SAT was one thing; this was something else. My skull was going to blow apart if I let it, but I forced myself through grim determination to keep it together.

Gobi glanced at me. "You are upset?"

"Upset? Am I upset?" Here all I needed was some hack cartoonist to reach down and draw steam shooting out of my ears. *"I never should have taken you to prom!"*

"Perry, listen to me. Tomorrow morning I will fly out."

"I thought it was next week—"

"It is tomorrow morning. Before that I have four more appointments I need to make here in the city. You drive me to these, everything will be all right."

"Four appointments. You mean four more people you have to kill?"

"Please pay attention to your driving."

I shook my head. "You know, it all makes total sense now why you weren't good in math. Every single foreign exchange student I know is good in math. You sucked in math because you're *actually a hired killer.*"

"Red light."

Slamming on the brakes, I stopped just short of getting T-boned by a bus heading east on Fourteenth Street. Gobi was still typing on the BlackBerry. I caught a glimpse of digitized information, photos, a Google map scrolling upward.

"So the whole time you were living with us, that was all a cover?" My mind flicked back to the nights where I'd heard her talking in Lithuanian, the hours she'd spent in front of her laptop. "The last nine months you were just getting the assignment together?"

"It is not an easy process." She lifted the BlackBerry. "The research was extensive."

47

"Who are they? The people you're killing?"

"Light is green."

That was when my cell phone started ringing. Gobi's eyes flashed down.

"Who is it?"

I picked up the phone, checked the number, and felt a slick dark cloud of nausea swooping down over me, eclipsing all thought.

"It's my dad," I said.

# 9

Describe a disappointment in your life and how
you responded. (Notre Dame)

"What . . . what do I do?"

We were coming into Union Square now, traffic looking worse
than bad, and all I could think was that my father would never have
wanted any of this for his car, or for his son, but mainly for his car.

"Get in the left lane," Gobi said. "Take Fourteenth Street around
the park, pick up Broadway the next block down."

"No, about my dad."

"What will you do if you don't answer?"

"He'll probably just keep calling."

"Then you need to pick it up and talk to him."

"I can't—" The phone slipped out of my hand and Gobi caught
it midair, switched on the speaker, and held it up to my face so that
I could keep both hands on the wheel, cutting off the cab behind
me on my way left. "Hello?"

"Perry?"

"Dad?"

"I hear car horns. Where are you?"

"We, ah . . ." I threw a frantic look at Gobi. She shook her head, which could have meant anything, but which I interpreted as *Improvise, stupid.* "We had to leave the prom. Some stuff happened."

"Some *stuff*? What are you talking about?"

"We're sort of in the city."

"What city? You're in *New York?*" His voice sharpened, becoming more angular with every syllable. "May I remind you that you're driving the Jaguar, Perry."

"Dad, I know . . . Look—Gobi asked me to take her to the city, and, uh—"

"I don't care if the ghost of Frank Sinatra extended you a personal invitation to Carnegie Hall," Dad said. "I want to know what you're doing, driving my car into New York without conferring with your mother and me?" The anger in his voice was a controlled burn. "Now I want you to listen to me very carefully. As quickly and as *safely* as possible, I want you to turn around and come home, right now, where we can discuss the consequences of your rash decision. Do you understand me? Perry?"

The light changed and I took a left onto Fourteenth Street. Before I could answer, Gobi took the phone away and brought it to her own ear. She was still on speaker.

"Hello? Mr. Stormaire? This is Gobija."

"Gobi, put Perry back on the phone, please. This is a private matter."

"Mr. Stormaire, you must understand something. Your son is a good boy. All his life, he has dedicated himself to making you proud of him." She gestured up ahead where Fourteenth fed back into Broadway, continuing downtown. "Tonight I asked him to show me the city one last time before I flew home."

"Gobi, no offense, but this doesn't involve you in the least." I could hear his temper slipping a notch and felt the tightening in my sphincter that always preceded the instinct to do whatever he said. "Now put my son back on the phone."

She actually seemed to think about it. "No."

*"No?"*

"Not until you apologize for the way you have treated him."

There was a second of silence, and my dad said, "Come again?"

"For nine months I see things in your home, Mr. Stormaire, and I watch how you treat your son. I see that you want the best for him, but you have crushed his spirit with your expectations, and you have discouraged him with your restrictions. Family is important, but it is not immune to the indifference of a cold-hearted parent."

"I see," my dad said. "And you're an expert on this, are you, Gobi? On my family?"

"I know that the man who does not put his family first places his own soul at peril. I have been watching and listening. And while that may not make me an expert, I would say that I know what I am speaking of." She shifted her weight around in the seat, and I saw her face, the way she was focused intently on the phone. "There is a proverb in my country, Mr. Stormaire: *The faithless husband poisons his family at the roots.*"

"The faithless . . ." My dad stopped. "Wait a second. What are you talking about?"

"I believe we understand each other. I hardly think we need to go into the specifics of your ongoing relationship with Madelyn Kelso, do we?"

It was quiet for a long time.

"Excuse me?" Dad said. "Did you say Madelyn Kelso?"

"You heard me."

"Now you listen here. I don't know what you're referring to, or what you think you know—"

"I am referring to the events of April sixteenth," Gobi said without so much as a pause for a breath. "And your business trip to San Diego on the twenty-eighth, as well as your weekend at the Hotel Monaco with Ms. Kelso in Chicago on May third. Would you like me to continue?"

"How do you know about that?"

"May I inform you that you are on speakerphone, Mr. Stormaire."

Dad didn't say anything for a long time. When he finally did, his voice sounded completely different, unfamiliar from any type of fatherly intonation I'd ever heard before. It sounded gut-punched, out of breath. "Perry?"

"Perry will be back in the morning, along with your precious automobile. Until then you will not call him or harass him in any way, or I assure you that my next phone call will be to *Mrs.* Stormaire. Do we understand each other?"

"Now just a moment." Dad's voice sounded hoarse. "I'd like to speak to my son for moment, please."

"He heard everything you just said."

"Gobi, please—"

"Later," Gobi said, and hung up, handing me back the phone. We were back on Broadway, and I just drove.

# 10

You've just written a 300-page autobiography. Send us page 217. (University of Pennsylvania)

Traffic loosened south of Union Square. Broadway fed down past restaurants and all-night groceries, flower shops and guys setting up tables on the sidewalks, selling knockoff purses and jewelry and bootleg DVDs. I kept my eyes straight ahead, not talking, until Gobi turned and glanced up at me.

"I am sorry you had to find out this way, Perry."

"He promised us that was over," I said.

My voice felt dead, even to me, like somebody talking in his sleep. Gobi didn't say anything, just kept her attention on the street ahead as we passed through the Lower East Side toward the Financial District, the concrete canyonlands where college funds and retirement money was gained and lost every day.

"That stuff you told him about Madelyn," I said, "that wasn't just a bluff, was it?"

She picked up her BlackBerry, tapped in keys. "Wiretapping your phones was a security precaution along with routine surveillance.

As part of the assignment, I had to secure the site, including your father's private line."

"That's not an answer," I said.

But it was.

# 11

Courage has been described as "grace under pressure." How would you describe it? (Ohio State University)

My sinuses felt like they were filling with hot molten lead, suffocating me from the inside. I was thinking about what my dad had told me back in his office. "'A man has obligations outside himself . . .'" I muttered. "That hypocritical piece of crap." My hands gripped the wheel hard enough to whiten my knuckles, but I didn't let go because I didn't want to see how badly they were shaking. "She's his personal assistant—can you believe that? The first time Mom caught him, he promised it would stop for good."

Gobi said nothing, lost in her BlackBerry. I let her go. I could feel the past swimming up behind me to swallow me up. It took me back to the night two years ago when I'd come home from the library and stepped on a piece of broken dish lying in the foyer. Mom had thrown three of them at Dad on his way out the door. There was a gash in it, just above the doorknob.

I'd found her sitting on the couch in the living room with a gin and tonic in her hand, staring at *Dancing with the Stars* with the sound off.

"She threw him out of the house," I told Gobi. "He went to stay at a hotel that night and when he came back he promised it would never happen again."

She shrugged. "Men are swine."

"Not all of us."

Gobi nodded at the next intersection. "Pull into the alleyway," she said. "We're here."



She glanced at the lit office window twelve floors off the street, then back at me. "Here," she murmured, leaning over to wrap the plastic handcuffs from her bag around my wrists.

"Wait, what's this?"

She looped the restraints through the Jaguar's steering wheel, cinching them to the skin.

"Ow, that's too tight!"

"Stay here."

"Like I could go anywhere?"

She reached into the bag and took out the gun I had seen earlier.

"Gobi, *wait*—"

She got out and sank into the shadows half a block off Pearl Street, a Lithuanian ninja. I jerked tentatively on the wrist restraints but that only made them tighter. She had left her bag sitting on the passenger seat, and I wondered what else she had in there—passports, more weapons, a bazooka?

I looked up to the rearview mirror, back up the alleyway to the street. I put both hands on the steering wheel and blasted the horn. It was ten fifteen. Somewhere over on Avenue A, Inchworm had started their sound check at Monty's. I hit the horn again. I imagined my dad wandering through the house with a scotch and soda in his hand, wondering how on earth a foreign exchange student had found out about his ongoing affair with his assistant. I blasted the horn again. Back in Boy Scouts we'd learned Morse code, and I tried to remember how to do SOS, but settled for a series of irregular, spastic-sounding honks, hoping it sounded desperate and not just like a malfunctioning car alarm or the drum part from "My Sharona," a song that Inchworm sometimes played at our live shows, but only ironically.

At the far end of the alley, a pair of headlights appeared.

"Thank you, God." I hit the horn in shorter, sharper blasts and started shouting out the open window. "Help! Help me! Up here!"

The headlights turned in and started toward me. Red and blue swirled from the roof as the cruiser pulled up directly behind me, doors opening.

The female officer who approached the car didn't look as if she were in a hurry.

"Is there a problem, sir?"

I jerked my head down at the plastic wrist restraints. "I'm tied to the wheel here."

"Yes, sir. I can see that."

"The woman who did it is up in that office building. She has a gun. She went up there to kill somebody. She's an assassin. Also, she's Lithuanian." Why this last part was important, I didn't know; maybe it added what the SAT might call verisimilitude.

"An assassin?" Now I had the cop's attention, but she seemed just as interested that I was seventeen years old, wearing a rented tuxedo, and driving a Jaguar that clearly didn't belong to me. Her flashlight went to the stamp on my right hand: UNDERAGE. She drew in a deep breath. "Is this some kind of joke?"

"There's blood on the windshield," I said. "Does that look like I'm joking?"

She raised her flashlight to the windshield and played it across the blood. That was when a bullet hole appeared in the glass. It was a brand new bullet hole, I realized; it had just happened.

The *pop* sound arrived afterward, like an afterthought. The cop went into a duck-and-cover position next to the Jaguar, grabbing her radio from her belt and saying cop things into it, shouting codes and signals. I heard the next bullet go whining off the cement next to her and she sprang back up, bounding off in the direction of her cruiser. Shots were spanging and spackling off the ground now like hail, and a second later Gobi came running back up to the car and jumped into the passenger seat with the gun in her hand. Blood flecked one side of her face and she was breathing hard, looking over her shoulder at the police car.

"You did it again, didn't you?" I asked. "You shot somebody else!"

"What were you doing?" she said, turning the ignition key. "Drive."

I hit the gas and sent us roaring blindly back down the alley, scraping past a dumpster and stacks of boxes, my hands still tied to the wheel. Before I could say anything, Gobi raised the butt of the pistol and whacked me across the back of the head.

"Ow! Shit! Crap!"

"All I ask you to do is wait! One simple thing! Only wait!"

"I didn't—"

She raised the gun again. I shut up, cringing back. She lowered the gun. "You put innocent lives in danger when you take stupid risks! What were you thinking?"

"Were you really going to shoot that cop?"

She looked back. The police lights were flashing up the alleyway after us, playing off puddles and brick walls. "I might still have to." She shook her head, gazing at me with a mixture of exasperation and annoyance. "I understand now why you never have a girlfriend, Perry."

"What? I've had a girlfriend! What's that got to do with anything?"

"You do not know how to listen to a woman." She pointed. "Out this way, take a right."

Tires screeching, I took the corner too fast, the back of the Jaguar fishtailing and caroming off the back of a newspaper stand. I hoped that she didn't lean out the window and start shooting back at the cop, but the very act of hoping seemed to bring that exact scenario to life, because seconds later Gobi was leaning out the window and shooting back at the cop.

"I've had lots of girlfriends," I shouted. It had just occurred to me that if Gobi was tapping the phone at our house then she might have been eavesdropping on my cell phone conversations too, and overheard the countless conversations in which Norrie had referred to my virginity, both explicitly—"Hello, Mr. Virgin"—and in not so-secret code—"Aye aye, Cap'n Cherry." Once, junior year, apropos of nothing, he'd interrupted the middle of our conversation comparing Wendy's and Fuddruckers with an entire song apparently composed on the spot, to the tune of "Like a Virgin":

> *Perry's a virgin.*
> *Never even touched a girl's slime.*
> *He's a vir-ir-ir-ir-gin.*
> *And he'll stay one, till the end of time.*

Gobi dispelled any doubt on this issue when she turned to me and said:

"But you still are a virgin."

"What? No! No, I'm not."

She stuck the gun back out the window and fired again. "I heard you talking about it on the phone."

"That's a total invasion of privacy! Besides, that was a joke. It's just a stupid nickname."

"Your nickname is Virgin?"

"Yeah, it's ironic, like when you call a big guy Tiny."

"So you have had many girls?"

"Many, yeah, a lot." I was giving myself whiplash trying to figure out what street we were on. It looked just like Pearl Street, except I thought we were a little farther north, in Tribeca—could that be right? Then the street opened up and I saw the September 11 Memorial Site straight ahead of me, Ground Zero, which seemed completely appropriate given that the police car behind me was about to pull me over, if Gobi didn't kill the cop first.

But the strobe lights behind us were gone.

"We lost them," I said. "Did we lose them? I think we lost them."

Gobi scowled into her side-view mirror. "We picked up a tail."

"What? I don't see anybody."

"Not the police this time. Black Humvee, six cars back."

"You can see that far?" I craned my neck but could only make out generic strings of headlights up and down the street. "Who is it?"

She didn't answer, consulting her BlackBerry. The look of worry on her face was new, more serious than before. It meant something, but she wasn't going to tell me. The light in front of me was turning red.

"Run it."

"I don't think—"

"Now."

I slammed the accelerator. At the exact same second, the Humvee that I hadn't seen before came charging out of the line of traffic behind us and into the right lane, accelerating fast until it was almost alongside the Jaguar. I was in the middle of the intersection now, shoved sideways on the cushion of displaced air that the Hummer had created upon its arrival, cabs blasting their horns, screeching their brakes to avoid hitting us. The Hummer growled through behind me, took a hungry bite out of a taxi's right bumper, and just kept coming, a living force of demonic automotive vengeance. The back window of the Jaguar exploded with a shotgun blast and I felt my blood jump in my veins. I think I screamed.

"They're shooting at us! *They're* shooting at *us!*"

"Turn left," Gobi said. "Down this alley. And hold your arms still." She flicked open a straight razor and cut off the restraints, bringing sudden, blessed relief. "Keep going."

I cranked the wheel hard, trying at the same time to look over my shoulder. "Who's in the Humvee?"

She didn't answer. I was going forty miles an hour down an empty alley, with the headlights off praying that there was nothing in front of me. At the far end I saw lights of some big street and knew already that I wasn't going to be able to stop and wait for a break in traffic. I was just going to have to hope there was nothing coming from either direction when I got there.

The Jaguar torpedoed out of the alleyway and I turned right because it was easier than turning left. We were on Avenue A somehow—my sense of Manhattan geography was hopelessly scrambled and I didn't know if we were heading uptown or downtown—and the Humvee was nowhere in sight. I felt the endorphins simmering in a stew of adrenaline, the whole soupy mess coming to a boil in my temples. My chest started aching and I realized that I hadn't breathed in the last twenty seconds.

"Are they gone?"

"For now."

I swung to the curb and hit the brakes hard enough that Gobi jerked forward in her seat. Her bag fell open and the gun slipped out.

It was one of those life moments, the kind that all future events pivot upon. Not even thinking, I grabbed it in both hands and pointed it at her. She seemed both surprised and impressed by the speed with which I'd managed to turn the tables.

"Not bad, Perry. You are learning."

"Shut up," I said. The gun was shaking in my hands, but I didn't care. "Get out of my car."

She didn't move. "Don't you mean your father's car?"

"Whatever. I don't know why you picked me for this, but I'm done, you understand? I'm *through*. I'm eighteen years old. In a month I'm going to graduate, I'm waitlisted at Columbia . . . and this—whatever it is—isn't part of the plan."

"So you are going to shoot me?"

"If I have to, yeah."

"All right."

"What?"

"Go ahead and do it. You have the gun. It is loaded." She waited. "But first you better take off the safety. It is the switch on the side. But you will not. Because you do not have the balls."

"You don't think so?"

"I know so."

"Well, you're wrong."

Keeping the gun pointed at her, I flipped the safety off. All at once I could hear the noise of the city, the traffic pulsing on the expressway, the subways roaring under the sidewalks, millions of people out talking and driving around, living their lives. I smelled coffee and cigarettes and perfume and wet trees, tasted it in the air. It was all incredibly alive, like my heart and lungs working on overload, resonating in my chest and pounding through my skull.

For an instant our eyes met and I saw that Gobi was smiling slightly, enjoying this.

And she said, "Wait."

# 12

What have you undertaken or done on your own in the last year or two that has nothing to do with academic work? (Northwestern)

"One thing that I must ask you, Perry, before you shoot me."

"Yeah? What's that?"

"Have you ever been to Europe?"

"What?"

"Have you ever traveled outside of your own country?"

I stared at her. "What's that got to do with anything?"

"Just answer the question."

"No, I . . . I've been to Canada, but that's about it."

"You should consider traveling, spending some time seeing the world. It's best when you're young."

"Okay," I said. "I'm going to shoot you now."

"Wait," she said. "One more thing."

"What?"

"I have wired sixty-five pounds of Tovex in the basement of your house."

"*What?*"

"If you shoot me and I do not make a phone call at a certain time, my contact will blow the charges by remote detonator and burn down your house with your family in it."

"That's insane! What if it goes off by accident?"

"My name is another form of Gabija, the goddess of fire in Lithuanian mythology," she said. "In my country it was said that when Gabija became angry she would take a walk and set fires wherever she went."

"You're a complete lunatic. How do you know it's just not going to go off all by itself?"

"I am trained in explosives, among other things."

"Oh, right, of course," I said, *Le Femme Gobija.*" The comparison, which was supposed to make me feel better, actually had the opposite effect, sandbagging my lower GI tract with a bout of sudden, hammering queasiness.

"May I have my gun back, if you are not going to shoot me with it?"

I hesitated, just for a second, and in that moment her hand flashed out, snapping the weapon from me in one neat twisting motion. I looked at my empty palm and open fingers. "You could have done that anytime you wanted."

"I wanted you to understand the stakes."

"How long have the explosives been in our basement?" I asked.

"About eight months," Gobi said, and then, of my amazed and horrified reaction: "I had to be sure, in case anything happened." She rested one hand on my forearm in a gesture that was probably meant to be reassuring. "Is okay. I will remove it in the morning before I leave."

"If we even survive that long," I said. We were still sitting on Avenue A, an island of stillness in a cavalcade of nighttime traffic.

"You know, I don't even see how you got through the exchange student screening process. Don't they do extensive background checks or something?"

"I seduced my admissions officer."

"Wonderful."

"She seemed to think so."

*"She?"*

Gobi reached over and squeezed my thigh. "Does that excite you?"

"No."

"You must learn to adapt, Perry. Improvise. Go with the flow."

"I almost went with the flow a second ago when you were shooting at that cop."

She slipped the gun back in her bag and glanced out the window, reorienting herself to our location. I got the sense that she was wired into the night itself, aware of every fluctuation of electricity and sound, the reflections in glass and steel. "We need to disappear for a while," she said. "Downtown is too hot for us now. Santamaria knows we are here."

"Who's Santamaria?"

"Santamaria sent those men in the black Humvee."

I shook my head. "I totally should have shot you when I had the chance."

"And the explosives?"

"I could have called my family and told them to get out of the house, then called the bomb squad."

"Ach," she said, and gave my leg another squeeze, this one not so gentle. "The explosives are wrapped in a charcoal filter to throw off the dogs. Also, you would have to call your father. And we already know how you feel about that."

Suddenly all the levity went out of her voice. From up the street I heard tires squealing. I twisted around and saw headlights streaking forward, etching across the darkness. Before I could even see the vehicle, I knew it would be the Humvee, bearing down on us from half a block away and closing in fast.

"They are here."

"What do we do?"

"Take the keys." Gobi flung out one arm, opened my door and shoved me out, swinging me forward toward a group of people standing at the intersection. We hit the ground at a dead sprint, keeping to the shadows. Just before we turned the corner, I looked back and saw the Hummer jerk to a halt alongside the now empty Jaguar, two figures jumping out to surround it on either side.

I was out of breath, trying not to gasp for air.

"Where are we going?" I managed.

"Somewhere friendly," she said. "Keep moving."

"Forget it." I stopped in my tracks. "I'm not going anywhere else with you."

"Then I will blow your house up," she said, without breaking stride. "Do you believe me?"

*Yes,* I thought.

"No."

"Then this is goodbye."

After a second, I ran to catch up.


Six blocks up Avenue A, I realized where she was taking me.

"Wait," I said, "we're going *here?*"

Gobi swung open the door of Monty's and pushed me in first, as if expecting an ambush. I stumbled inside and got my bearings—if that was even possible in a place like this.

Depending on who you asked, Monty's was either an irredeemable dump or the last of the great East Village rock clubs left over from the eighties. That last bit came directly from the owner, a Norwegian recovered junkie named Sven that none of us had actually met and who possibly existed only as part of the club's lore. Supposedly Sven's brother-in-law had set up Inchworm's show and cashed the $2500 check Norrie and I had written last fall when we first set up the show, because that was the way it worked: you bought the place out for the night and hoped people showed up and paid at the door. We'd all read Legs McNeil's *Please Kill Me* from cover to cover and were thrilled to be taken advantage of in such a historic fashion.

Gobi pointed at the Xeroxed Inchworm flyer stapled inside the doorway. I recognized it immediately—it was the one that Norrie and I had printed and plastered around town last weekend.

"Your band is playing here tonight," she said. "It is a good cover for us until things cool off."

"Wait," I said. "You're using my gig as your hideout?"

"What is the matter, Perry? Do you feel *exploited?*"

"I liked you better when you were this geeky quiet exchange student."

"Well, perhaps I liked you better when you just shut your mouth and stared at my chest," she said, "but we cannot always get what we want in this world."

"I never . . . I didn't—"

"You are expected to be here tonight. Everybody knows that. And so you get up, play your songs, buy us some time." She shrugged. "It is not the best cover, but it will hold for now."

I started to argue again, but Gobi cut me off with the sweep of her hand, as if such things were beneath explanation, especially to one as slow-witted as myself. To my left, the bouncer, a shriveled, capuchin-faced gnome in the hoodie, gave me an indifferent blink. "Five dollars."

"I'm in the band," I muttered. "Perry Stormaire."

"Not on the list."

"That's because I'm *in the band.*"

"Not on the list."

I opened my wallet and found ten dollars, handing it over. It was my last ten dollars.

"ID?"

Holding up my hand, I showed him the UNDERAGE stamp from the 40/40 Club.

"No alcohol," the gnome said. "You can't—"

"Sit at the bar, yeah, I know."

He waved us forward, making a point of checking Gobi out as she sauntered by. A moment later I heard a staticky blurt of microphone noise, and up on stage, I saw Norrie, along with Caleb and our lead singer, Sasha, marching out, gazing at the crowd with a combination of carefully feigned rock-and-roll disregard and barely controlled panic. They hadn't seen me yet.

"Gobi," I said, a terrible possibility occurring to me. "Wait. You're not going to kill anybody here, are you?"

"Not unless is absolutely necessary." She paused and took a speculative look at the band. "In firefight, would any of them take a bullet for you, do you think?" Her eyes lingered on Norrie. "The one in back, perhaps playing the drums—he is good size, and would make a good shield, if it came to that."

"You're kidding, right? Are you kidding? That's my best friend." My mind was still reeling, trying to imagine a scenario more desperate than being gunned down at my band's first real New York gig, when I felt a hand grasp my shoulder.

As Gobi slipped into the crowd, I turned around and looked at the two adults standing in front of me.

"Mom?" I said. *"Dad?"*

# 13

It has been said that "in the future everyone will be famous for fifteen minutes" (Andy Warhol). Describe your fifteen minutes. (New York University)

Staring at them, I realized that forty-five minutes had passed since I'd spoken to my father on the phone.

"We thought we might find you here," he said, raising one hand like he might pat me on the back or haul off and sock me in the jaw. In the end he just let the hand flop back to his side. He was looking at me very closely, with an intensity I'd never seen before and didn't particularly like. It made my skin itch. "I suppose Gobi's here with you?"

"She's . . . somewhere," I said.

Dad nodded and started scanning the crowd. I imagined his Terminator-vision analyzing the faces for some trace of the woman with the sole power to bring down his marriage.

"Perry," Mom said, "how could you do this to us? How could you betray our trust?"

"*Me* betray your trust?" I looked back over at Dad. "Mom—"

"*Good evening, New York!*" Sasha bellowed from the stage, loud enough to startle everybody, spilling a few drinks and momentarily souring the communal mood. *"I heard New York City wants to rock!"*

There was a momentary lull as the crowd looked up, judged Sasha not to be an immediate threat, and went back to their drinks and conversations.

*"I said,"* Sasha insisted, *"that I heard New York City wants to rock!"*

It wasn't exactly clear why we'd taken Sasha on as Inchworm's lead singer. On the plus side, he did have that element of raw animal savagery vital to a frontman. On the other hand, he seemed to think this was 1985, when his parents had been his age.

With the downtown crowd continuing to ignore him, Sasha decided to give formal notice that the show was about to begin. He communicated this by executing a flying roundhouse kick, letting out a Comanche warrior's shriek, and picking up a Stratocaster, an instrument I'd seen him play only when he was drinking tequila and the guitar itself was invisible. Meanwhile, behind him, Norrie attacked the bass. Caleb, normally our lead guitarist, had settled himself behind the drums.

That was when I realized that in my absence, Norrie had reassigned instruments. The only reason I recognized the results—a cover of Motley Crüe's "Kickstart My Heart"—was that we'd planned on opening with it.

The crowd responded by continuing to ignore them, slightly more aggressively.

Remembering the plastic explosives in the basement of my house, I turned back to my mother, who appeared to be on the verge of tears. "Mom, where's Annie?"

"What?"

*"Where's Annie?"*

"She's at home."

"In the house?"

"Yes, Perry, that's usually where people are when they're at home."

"You need to call her and tell her to get out of there, right now!"

"I can't hear you over this racket!"

"I said—"

Dad appeared between us, blocking Mom out entirely. He leaned in close so that I could hear him. "Perry. We need to talk."

"Dad—"

"Those things that Gobi was talking about, I don't know where she heard them or what she thinks she knows, but those were legitimate business trips."

"Dad," I said, "you're obviously lying, but right now I couldn't care less."

Holy shit—had I just said that? I was still trying to figure out whether the actual words had left my lips when my dad grabbed me by my tuxedo shirt and shook me, slightly harder than I'd expected. I knew that he went to the gym, but he was also fifty-two years old and his favorite foods were bourbon and bacon.

"Now you listen to me," he said. "I'm your father and right now you are *way* off the reservation on this one—you understand?"

Over his shoulder I saw Gobi come out of the crowd. She froze and looked at us, and I saw she was holding what looked like a taser, pointing it at my dad's neck. I shook my head sharply.

"No?" Dad asked, misinterpreting my head shake. "Well, let me make it crystal clear. As long as you live under my roof, you will obey certain rules. You're not a child anymore. Your music, this little game you play, is over. It's time to focus on more pressing matters."

I glanced back at Gobi again. A man in a leather jacket had appeared behind her. He was probably in his twenties, and his face looked like a sculpture made by a disturbed metal-shop student with a fondness for veins. His haircut was shellacked with gel product, giving it the resinous, bulletproof appearance of a Ken doll's. At that exact same moment, a second man, the same age, with eyes cut out of the same semicolorless agate, materialized to my immediate right. He wore a barn coat and his shoulders gave him the tight, heavy look of a man who'd done prison time, maybe a lot of it. A teardrop tattoo was suspended under his left eye. There was a density about both of them that made me think of guns concealed under layers of Teflon and Kevlar.

I thought instantly about the black Humvee.

"Are you even listening to me?" Dad asked. "I'm *talking* to you."

"Dad, we have to get out of here."

I looked for Gobi, but she had vanished. But not Teardrop Tattoo. He was striding straight toward me with an expression of dawning purpose, as if every nagging uncertainty in his life, every unresolved question and crisis of faith, had been answered in the form of the idea of kicking my ass. He shoved my dad aside without even looking at him, and my dad, for his part, went over without a bit of resistance.

Teardrop Tattoo locked eyes with me, and I saw my own death reflected there. It was not heroic or meaningful or even particularly interesting, just bloody, painful, awkward, and agonizing. I looked back at the stage where the ragged, awful noise that wasn't music had already started dissolving into a bowlegged twang of strings and random cymbal taps, like a stoned octopus slithering through a Guitar Center.

Teardrop Tattoo charged me.

With no place else to go, I jumped up onto the stage.

\*     \*     \*

As soon as I got up there and Norrie realized what was happening —
*"Holy shit! It's Perry!"*— the band instantly re-reorganized. I grabbed
the bass and Sasha tossed his guitar to Caleb, who abandoned the
drums for Norrie, who clicked his sticks together, firing off a
four-count for our original song "It's My Funeral." At first I didn't
think I'd even be able to play—I had way too much going on in my
mind—but to my profound surprise, my fingers didn't seem to care.
Apparently if you wanted to rock, it didn't matter if you had explosives in the basement, or a father with a chronic problem with keeping his dick in his pants, or a crazed ex-Blackwater employee with
some religious conviction for ripping your head off.

Hell, it might have *helped.*

In the beginning the crowd regarded us with the distracted curi-
osity you might pay to a three-legged dog hobbling down the other
side of the street. Twenty seconds later, though, most of them had
stopped what they were doing and just watched us. By then people
were actually nodding along with the music. We finished the song
and the cheering started.

"Dude!" Norrie shouted, gesturing me over to the drums. Sweat
was pouring from him in rivers and streams, soaking his gray Fugazi
T-shirt black around the neck and pits and painting a long black
dagger down his spine. The grin on his face made him look about
six years old. "You made it! That was awesome!"

Backing away, ignoring him completely, I scanned the crowd for
Teardrop Tattoo and saw him standing at the foot of the stage,
brain-raping me with his eyes. As long as we kept playing, he couldn't
touch me. "Hey, Norrie, look—"

"Whoa, man." Norrie grabbed my arm. "Did you see who's out
in the crowd?"

"Who, my dad?"

"Jimmy Iovine. That's J-Jimmy freakin' *Iovine*, dude."

"Really?"

"Yeah, man, check it out. It's t-totally him." An elbow as sharp as a Dungeons and Dragons broadsword dug into my ribs. "I *t-told* you Interscope was s-stalking our Facebook page. Y-Y-You thought it was b-bullshit, but there he is." Norrie's I'm-six-at-Disney-World smile was now a huge, goofy chimpanzee grin that stretched out both sides of his face like a cut-rate facelift. "This is it. This is *so* our t-t-time, right now."

"Okay." *Breathe, asshole,* I told myself. Teardrop Tattoo was now gripping the stage in front of me as if he was considering jumping up on it.

And then, just when the moment couldn't possibly get any weirder, I saw another familiar face in the crowd, a tall, cool brunette at the far end of the room.

Valerie Statham had come to my rock-and-roll show.

I looked at Norrie. "My dad's boss is here."

"What?"

"The one who's supposed to write my letter of recommendation to Columbia. I forgot that I invited her to the show." I could suddenly feel the unmistakable sensation of my two different worlds colliding in my brain. "What do we do?"

"Wh-What the hell do you think we do?" Norrie grinned. "W-W-We rock harder than we ever have in our lives."

"What song?"

"I think it has to be 'Tovah.'"

I was simultaneously hoping he'd say that and praying that he wouldn't. "Tovah" was the song we'd been working on for the past two months. It was about a girl that Norrie had met and fallen in love with at Jewish camp when he was fourteen years old, who had died of an overdose of Valium and tequila the following year, and when it was finished, it might turn out to be the best thing we'd ever written together, but it wasn't finished.

In the end, that didn't really matter.

We ripped into it hard and the people responded instantly, just lit up like the JumboTron in Times Square. It was as if up till now we'd been serving ginger ale and we'd suddenly switched to Jack Daniel's. The guy at the bar who might have been Jimmy Iovine put his phone down and started listening. Valerie Statham turned and stared. Even Teardrop Tattoo looked impressed. We finished the second verse and went into the chorus—

And the world went black.

# 14

Reflect on these words of Dorothy Day: "No one has the right to sit down and feel hopeless. There's too much work to do." What is "the work to be done" for your generation, and what impact does this have on your future as a leader? Write a creative, reflective, or provocative essay. (Notre Dame)

The sound died with the lights, a candle blown out with a single puff. For a second I could hear Sasha's voice in the dark, squalling naked and childlike without the aid of a microphone, and then Norrie's drums rattled silent. The crowd reacted instantly with a startled last-episode-of-*Sopranos* "Huh?" of shock and confusion.

I felt a hand grab my sleeve and jerk me from the stage. I dropped my bass and swung my arms out to catch myself, experiencing air's notorious inadequacy when it comes to behaving as a solid, and then my chin slammed into the floor and my face went numb up all the way back to my jawbone.

"Get up," Gobi's voice hissed in my ear, with all the rage of a culturally repressed eastern Europe behind her words, but by that point she was already dragging me through the crowd. Scrambling to my feet, I went staggering through the front door and outside into the night.

"What are you doing?"

"Saving your life."

"Now?"

"We must go."

I looked back at the club. "But we were rocking!"

"Too many people paying attention," she said.

"That's kind of the p—"

"Shut up." She jabbed something into the small of my back and we walked quickly back up Avenue A toward the park. The sight of the Jaguar seemed to reassure her. "Get in."

I opened the driver's side door and heaved myself in, still dizzy and sweating. "You couldn't have at least waited till we finished the song? One of the most important guys in the music industry was sitting at the bar."

"Does not matter," Gobi said, consulting her BlackBerry.

"Maybe not to you, but it matters to me."

"That is not what I mean." She turned to face me. "I saw you with your father at that club. All he has to do is tell you to stop, and just like that you give up your dreams, like poof, like they were nothing."

"We were *good* up there."

Gobi smiled at me. She had the strangest way of doing that at odd moments.

"You were better than good, Perry. You were great."

"Thanks."

"It is just a pity that you cannot stand up for what you love."

"What, like killing people for money?"

Gobi stiffened. A flat, dispassionate mask clamped over her face, and her voice went flat.

"Drive uptown," she said. "Should take no more than fifteen minutes."

# 15

Are you honorable? How do you know? (University of Virginia)

It was almost eleven when we drove up Fifth Avenue and Gobi pointed to the entrance of the Sherry-Netherland Hotel. The valet in a red jacket and pants with gold piping approached the Jaguar and stopped, inspecting the body damage, the smashed rear window, and the blood on the windshield. His face went from a placatory smile to the "Oh, no" emoticon of ☹.

"Is everything all right, sir?"

I nodded and kept my eyes on Gobi. She had my cell phone in her bag, but as soon as she got out, I was going to do whatever I could to get in touch with Annie and make sure she was safely out of the house. Then I was going to bolt.

"Come on." She gestured me out. "This time you are coming with me."

"I'd rather stay put, thanks."

She reached in and pulled me out. How a girl that weighed fifty pounds less than me could force me out of a vehicle and make it look elegant was a total mystery, but the valet appeared to find it amusing, almost ☺. He was still beaming at us as Gobi held my arm and swung me into the hotel lobby.

"What am I supposed to do?"

"Shut up. Be charming."

We walked toward the hotel bar, a place called Harry Cipriani's. It was a loud, lemon-colored room with lacquered wooden walls, full of low tables clustered together everywhere like toadstools. The air smelled like seafood and split-pea soup. Gobi went into stealth mode, assessing the patrons, until her gaze came to rest on an old man in a gray vintage tuxedo and a great cloud of wintry white hair, surrounded by several carafes of wine and a pile of dirty saucers. He had red, scaly ears that stuck almost straight out from his head, and he was pushing his long nose into a red wine glass, sniffing repeatedly and shaking his head, muttering under his breath, a comedic performance. Flanking him were two giggling young women that could have been his granddaughters but probably weren't.

Gobi stood and waited while he looked up at her.

"Hello?" His voice had a heavy Slavic accent that made it sound lower and more suspicious than he probably was. "What is it? Do we know each other?"

"We might," Gobi said. "You are Milos Lazarova?"

Now the suspicion sounded more genuine. "Who are you?"

"So quickly you forget?" Gobi smiled, and I could almost hear the twinkle in her voice. "Your granddaughter Daniela and I were at university together in Prague. We had Christmas dinner at your palazzo in Rome. Surely you haven't forgotten me so soon."

The old man gazed at her deeply and then shook his head, looking both flummoxed and charmed. "Forgive me. For the life of me, I cannot recall your name."

"Tatiana Kazlauskieni." Gobi offered her hand, and Milos kissed it.

"Please, sit." He turned his gaze to me, and without a word the two bimbo bookends that had been sitting on either side of him abruptly stood up and vanished. "You must introduce me to your lucky friend."

Gobi smiled. "This is Perry. My fiancée."

"Doubly lucky, then," Milos said, beaming, and gestured to the suddenly vacant chairs. "You must both join me. I insist."

"We really can't—"

"Thank you, how kind." Gobi jammed something hard into my spine, an elbow or a dagger or the barrel of a gun, and I sat down heavily, still feeling the old man's eyes on me. They were as brown as chestnuts, searching and soulful, with the depth of those of someone who'd lost something close to him and had never quite allowed himself to get over it.

"The specialty of the house is the Bellini." Milos raised three fingers at a waiter without glancing away from us. "You must try it. Surely you know the origin of this bar."

"I do not," Gobi said. Her eyes sparkled. "You must enlighten me."

"Harry Cipriani is a near duplicate of Harry's Bar in Venice, famous watering hole of many American luminaries." Milos smiled, radiating a luxuriant, liquid happiness that seemed to saturate this entire corner of the bar. "In the early 1950s, I was down and out in Venice, living like a peasant." A slight nostalgic smile played at the corner of his lips. "I had just come to the end of an affair with a married woman, much to the ire of her husband, who happened to be a very influential Venetian businessman. Suffice it to say, it had not ended well for me." He chuckled, deep in the memory now, far beyond reach. "In any case, I walked into the Harry's Bar hoping for a glass of water and a crust of bread. I had perhaps five hundred lira in my pocket—the one pocket that did not have a hole in it. I half expected them to throw me out on the street." His eyes flicked upward for just a second, then returned to us. "When I walked in, there was an American holding court at the bar, a big bear of a man with a beard and a loud voice, surrounded by several reporters and sycophants. He looked familiar, but I couldn't place him. When he noticed me standing there in my shabby clothes, waiting to get the bartender's attention, he stopped in the middle of the story and asked who I was. I told him that I was no one, just a young man down on his luck. The loud American smiled—smiled with his eyes, you know, as if recognizing a kindred spirit. 'That kind of luck only comes from a woman,' he said, and he bought me my first Bellini."

I looked at him, remembering last year's English class, when we'd read *A Moveable Feast*. "Was it Ernest Hemingway?" I asked.

"In the flesh," Milos beamed. "He invited me to join him, and the two of us spent the rest of the afternoon drinking and talking about women. He seemed intensely interested in my experiences with the fairer sex, few though they were. 'A young man's distractions are far more potent than an old man's memories,' he told me. He said that in the end memory is a cheat and a lie and no substitute for what he called the real stuff, the stuff of life."

Milos straightened up, resurfacing from half a century ago. He appeared thirty years younger, the beneficiary of some rejuvenation formula.

"And now we drink our Bellinis."

Exactly on cue, the white-jacketed waiter delivered three champagne flutes full of sparkling pink purée, setting them down in front of us. What was inside was cold enough to fog the glass. Gobi raised hers to her lips, and Milos lifted his. I reached out and picked mine up, sure that I was going to knock it over, although somehow I managed not to. Apparently when Milos was ordering the drinks, the UNDERAGE stamp on my hand didn't mean squat.

"Speaking of the stuff of life . . ." He gestured, and when I looked around I saw that the waiters had cleared the tables away, creating an open space in the middle of the floor. Milos smiled at Gobi. "Will you two dance?"

That was when I realized that tango music had started playing from recessed speakers in the ceiling, and several couples were already beginning to slide easily through the newfound space. Before I could say anything, Gobi took my hand and pulled me up. I reached back and polished off my Bellini in one cold gulp.

"I can't dance, remember?" I whispered.

"It's just a tango. It is like sex, except with clothes on." Then, squeezing me closer. "Oh, I'm sorry. I forgot, you do not know how to do that either."

"Oh, ha-ha."

"Relax. Just follow my lead."

I glanced back at Milos watching us from his table. "You can't kill that guy. He's this sweet old European man. He didn't *do* anything."

"Shut up."

"He got hammered with Hemingway, for crying out loud."

"Hush." Her body moved against me, shifting and pressing; her eyes locked on mine. The alcohol had begun to swim up my bloodstream, warming me from the inside, and her thigh grazed my leg as the music swelled. At this proximity I noticed a detail that I'd never seen before, a thin streak of white scar tissue directly across her throat.

"Hold me tighter." She reached back and pinched my butt, hard. "You see?"

"Ow!"

"Come on. I won't break."

I yanked tight. "How's that?"

"Yes. That's it." She smiled a little and bit her lip. "You *are* improving." We swung around sideways and I caught another glimpse of Milos at his table. He had his cell phone out now and was still watching us with hooded, expressionless eyes. Then he was gone again as we revolved the other direction, and Gobi was all that I could see.

"Not bad for your first time," she said. "All you need is the right teacher."

"That's you?"

"It could be." She cocked one eyebrow. "Unless there is something you wish to teach *me*—in which case you had better make it fast." Another tiny smile: "Being your first time, I suppose it will be." She was rubbing up against me again, the friction close and rhythmic until I felt something building down there. "Is your safety off?"

"I don't have the gun, remember?"

"Are you sure?" She reached down, gripped me. "Oh. I *see*."

"You better stop doing . . . that . . ." I got out, not sure where I was going from there, and that was when she let me go, abruptly stepping back. Out of the corner of my eye, I saw Milos rising up from his chair. He was moving with surprising quickness for a man of his age, his hand jammed into his jacket pocket as he crossed the floor to Gobi.

"What is your real name?"

"Gobija Zaksauskas."

All remaining color drained from his face. At the same second he went absolutely rigid, the name reverberating through him visibly like a shock wave. "That's not possible. She's—"

Gobi took hold of his shoulders, spinning him around to the music. To anyone watching, she had simply changed partners. "Hemingway was an ugly American," she murmured, "but he was right about one thing." Her automatic appeared in her right hand, wedged into the old man's stomach just above his cummerbund, where only I could see it. "This kind of luck always comes from a woman."

"Please," the old man managed. "We can discuss this."

Gobi shook her head, turning him again. "There is nothing to discuss."

"I can explain. Just . . . tell me who sent you. What happened was regrettable."

*"Regrettable?"*

"Arrangements can be made. I don't know who is paying you—I can make you a better offer, I assure you."

"Can you offer me a pound of flesh?"

The old man's eyelids fluttered, not understanding. "What?"

"Take this." Gobi's left hand flipped out a butterfly knife. "Cut a pound of flesh from your body. You do that, and I'll let you live."

The old man looked at the knife. He reached up slowly, his hand trembling, rheumy eyes searching for someone, somewhere, to take him away from all of this. "Please," he said. "*Signorina,* whoever you are, I beg you, be reasonable."

"We're far beyond that point now."

"But—"

She shoved the knife deep into the center of the old man's abdomen, jerking it upward. He opened his mouth, blood spurting out over his lips, and Gobi clapped her hand over it, pressing him backwards as she yanked the blade out and wrapped a tablecloth around his waist, blocking his body from view as she let him sink to the floor. The whole thing took probably three seconds.

"Too many Bellinis," she murmured, and wiped the knife off on the tablecloth before turning back to me. "Go get the car."

# 16

In one page or less, describe an impossible scenario, real or hypothetical, and how you would respond to it. (Brandeis)

"Almost midnight," she said, climbing into the passenger seat. "We are ahead of schedule. Head uptown. East Eighty-Fifth Street." She turned to look at me. "What are you doing?"

I wasn't exactly sure. I knew that I'd staggered back out to the curb with my valet ticket and gotten the car and I was behind the wheel again, but now I seemed to be frozen in place. The image of the old man dying was burned so deeply into my corneas that it eclipsed all of Fifth Avenue and Central Park, and I couldn't seem to move.

The commotion in the bar was already spilling back out into the hotel lobby, growing louder by the second.

"Perry, now! Go!"

"Blood came out of his mouth," I said.

"What?"

"When you stabbed him. It was like he was puking blood. Like a fountain."

"That is because I severed his abdominal aorta," she said, as emotionless as an anatomy instructor. "Now can we please get out of here?" She retrieved her BlackBerry from her bag and started tapping keys.

I grabbed it.

# 17

In a moment of crisis, you have one phone call.
Whom do you call? (Grinnell College)

The element of surprise worked in my favor, at least long enough
for me to jump out of the car and run into the middle of Fifth Avenue, where I was almost hit by a limousine. I kept going, heading
for the park. I didn't turn and I didn't look back, just pounding hard
and fast for some other place where Gobi couldn't get me.

*The park,* I thought—the park was safe. There were trees, rocks,
water, none of the city elements that she'd be able to use to her favor.
I had the BlackBerry in my hand and was trying to dial while I ran,
which was almost impossible—but if I could hide somewhere long
enough, then maybe I could call home, and the police.

Bursting through the grass, I ran past the pond and headed
straight on through the darkness. I passed a jogger and startled some
ducks, sending them flapping and squawking skyward. There was a
pile of rocks up ahead, and maybe enough ground coverage to make a
call. I scrambled up, clutching Gobi's phone, trying not to make too
much noise as I panted for breath.

At the top, I stopped and looked back.

From here, the park looked empty.

I sucked in a deep, rib-aching breath and listened to the faint noises of the city filtering through the trees: voices, car horns, the horses from hansom cabs clip-clopping up along Central Park South. I inhaled New York and breathed out Perry Stormaire. The world smelled like budding leaves, algae, and fresh-cut grass. Given a moment of calm and sufficient oxygen, my mind flooded with images and jumbled thoughts. The old man choking on his own blood as he sloped to the floor of the bar . . . Gobi clutching me tightly and staring right into my eyes . . . the way that Milos had jerked backwards and gone pale when she gave her name. What had he meant about things being "regrettable"? How had he known her?

Keeping absolutely silent, I looked back down the walkway and saw nothing but trees and grass and the shimmering darkness of the pond. The traffic on Fifth Avenue was a world away. The loudest noise was the thudding of my own pulse, pushing on my eardrums. Looking up, I realized that I could see my dad's office building rising way up on Third Avenue. There were lights on at the top, one of the partners working late in the corner office.

I touched a button on the phone. The screen lit up instantly, casting a glow on my face. I dialed my home number and waited while it rang and rang.

Finally, Annie's voice answered:

"Hello?"

"Munchkin," I whispered. I could hear the TV in the background, music playing. She'd been listening to a lot of hip-hop and R&B since she'd turned twelve. "It's me."

"*Perry?* Where are you? Mom and Dad went to the city looking for you and Dad's super pi—"

"Annie, listen to me. You have to get out of the house, right now."

"What? Why?"

"It's not safe in there. You have to get out. Go to the Espenshades' down the street—just get out of there."

"Perry, it's like, midnight. I promised Mom I wouldn't leave the house. I'm not even supposed to answer the phone unless it's an emergency, and I'm like, how am I supposed to know it's an emergency unless I answer it, you know?" I heard her crunching on something, popcorn or nachos, followed by a slurp of soda. It made me feel better, knowing that she'd raided the pantry and was hanging out, alive, eating nachos. "Anyway, what are you doin'? You sound out of breath. Are you still in New York?"

"Annie, listen. There's a bomb in the basement."

"A what?"

"A bomb in the basement of our house."

"Ha-ha, very funny."

"I'm not joking. Gobi put it there."

"*Gobi?* Our foreign exchange student?"

"She's not a foreign exchange student—she's some kind of international assassin, and you have to get out of there, do you understand me?"

It was quiet for a long time, and the TV and music went away. Annie had either turned them off or gone into another room and shut the door.

"Munchkin? Are you still there?"

She breathed.

*"Annie?"*

"Do you promise this isn't some trick, Perry?" she said. "Because if it is, it's *really* mean."

"It's not a trick," I said.

"You swear?"

"I swear," I said. "Just get out of there."

"Okay."

"And call the police as soon as you get to the Espenshades'."

"Perry?"

"What?"

"I heard Gobi talking one night in her room when she didn't think anybody was there. I think she might have been talking about guns. She kept switching from English to Lithuanian. I didn't say anything because I thought I must have been hearing her wrong." Annie's voice warbled toward tears. "I'm kind of scared, Perry."

"Are you outside the house yet?"

"Yeah . . ."

"On the cordless?"

"Uh-huh . . ."

"Just keep walking," I said. "Get as far away from the house as you can. I'm going to stay on the phone till you get to the Espenshades' front door, okay?" I waited. "Annie?"

No answer. Had we lost the signal? Then I heard the sound of a car's motor getting louder.

"Annie, can you hear—"

"It's Mom and Dad!" Annie's voice burst out suddenly, full of relief. "Oh, Perry, they're *home!* They're back! It's okay!"

"Annie, wait! Tell them not to go in the—"

She was already gone.

# 18

What invention would the world be better off
without, and why? (Kalamazoo College)

I held up the phone, looking for the redial button.

From down below, at the bottom of the rock pile, I heard a click.

"Come down, Perry," Gobi said.

*Shit.*

"So are you going to kill me?" I asked.

"I do not want to." She stepped into the cast of a streetlight, her
shadow stretched out behind her along the sidewalk like something
cut from black felt by a pair of very sharp scissors. She was still carrying her big bag with her, dangling from one shoulder. The gun in
her other hand was pointed straight at my head. "But you know I
will if I have to."

"Then I might as well make it worth your while," I said, and
I lifted her BlackBerry up and flung it as hard as I could toward
the pond.

# 19

Are we alone? (Tufts)

Watch it fly.

A small thing, the weight of a pigeon, five ounces of circuitry and technology pinwheeling through the night air, screen glinting briefly as it arced downward toward the water and disappeared. *Plip.* Not even a splash. A duck quacked once and flapped away—Requiem for a BlackBerry.

I watched the ripples spread, reflecting the city lights.

Gone.

The next thing I heard was Gobi scaling the rocks toward me, scraping and clamoring up like a force of nature. I was halfway down the other side when she grabbed me by the throat and pulled me in, our mouths close enough that I felt her hair brush against my face.

"You have caused me a great deal of unnecessary difficulty tonight, Perry."

"Gee, you know, I'm really sorry. Maybe if you hadn't dragged me along on this whole thing, it wouldn't have been such an inconvenience for you."

Her other arm snapped across my elbow, hooking me close and

marching me back through the park to the pond. As we passed the pond, Gobi glanced over and shook her head. "That BlackBerry was my . . . How do you say? Lifeline."

"So . . . done for the night then?"

"Not even close."

Stepping back out onto Fifth Avenue, we stopped and looked back at the Sherry-Netherland. My dad's Jag was exactly where I'd left it in front of the hotel. Except now there were two NYPD cruisers parked in front and behind it, rolling their lights. An ambulance had pulled up in front of the canopied entrance, and it didn't take a psychic to guess the identity of the body being carried out on the litter. A small crowd of midnight gawkers had gathered under the clock. New York City had rubberneckers even at this time of night, I guessed, and they didn't seem to care who knew it.

"First the BlackBerry and now the car," Gobi said. "You are on a roll, Perry."

I tried to shrug again but couldn't pull it off. My shoulders felt fastened into place with a set of rusty bolts. Gobi stepped to the curb and hailed a cab.

"Brooklyn," she told the driver as she tossed the bag into the back and climbed in next to it. "Red Hook."

The cabbie started the meter and we swung into traffic.

"I thought we were going uptown," I said.

"That was before you interfered with my plans," Gobi whispered, not looking at me, leaning just enough that I could hear her. "Tonight was the only night that all five of my targets are going to be in the city. You have created another mess that needs taking care of. And this time you can take care of it yourself."

We rode along in silence, each lost in our own thoughts. I thought about Annie and my parents and wondered how they would react to what she told them about the bomb in the basement. I imagined my mom wanting to call the police and my dad dismissing the whole thing as ridiculous. He would probably march right down to the boiler room himself with a flashlight just to prove a point. When he actually found something—

*Wait.*

Annie had seen headlights pulling into our driveway and started running toward them. But what if it had been someone else? I assumed the men in the Hummer had the license plate number on the Jaguar. How long would it take to get my home address?

"We have to get back to Connecticut," I said. "Right now."

"That is impossible."

"Don't you get it? What if those two assholes in the Humvee decide to go up to my house and grab my sister?"

"They won't."

"How do you know that?"

"Because tonight their only orders are to kill us." She stared out the window, and I saw her reflection in the glass, pale and expressionless. "Me."

"Gobi."

"What is it?"

"That guy back at the hotel—when you told him that was your name, he looked like he'd seen a ghost."

No reply.

"He said that you being there was impossible," I said. "What did that mean?" I thought of the scar I'd seen across her throat when we were dancing, thread thin, like a flesh-colored choker underlying the half-heart pendant necklace that she was still wearing. "Who are you?"

She didn't budge.

"Damn it, talk to me. *Who are you?*"

Now she looked back at me, her green eyes full and hard and very bright.

"I am Death."

I felt an inward shudder pass over me, a reflexive tremor of dread. The first time I tried to speak, my throat was too dry and I had to swallow twice just to get enough moisture to form words. "What's that supposed to mean?"

"You are in no position to question me, Perry." Her voice was brittle. "You must think of your family."

"Believe me, I am."

"Then for now at least, you will do as I say."

I thought about my little sister, alone in the house and frightened, and the two men with cropped military haircuts, how they had come after us downtown, and my fear crackled up into a sharp orange flame of fury. "You should never have brought my family into this. You had no right to do that."

"I did what was necessary."

"Putting Annie's life in danger? How does that help the plan?"

"It was an insurance policy, nothing more. Everything else is just a cover."

"What about when we were dancing?" I said. "Was that just part of the cover too?"

She turned back to the window, the lights of the city playing across our faces as the cab cut through the night.

"Gobi."

But she didn't look over again.

# 20

If you could be a "fly on the wall" in any situation—historical, personal, or otherwise—describe what you would choose to observe and why. What would you hope to learn and how would it benefit you? (University of Pittsburgh)

It was after midnight down at the waterfront in Red Hook when she told the cabbie to drop us off in front of a flat-faced brick building that looked as if it could have been a shoe factory from sixty years ago. It had since either been turned into an expensive piece of yuppie housing or left alone to die a substandard housing project—from here it was impossible to tell. Deserted streets and empty basketball courts with torn nets surrounded us. I found myself staring back across the bay at the Statue of Liberty. It looked like it was made of Legos.

Gobi put down her bag and pointed.

"Through there," she said, and I followed her gesture to a wrought-iron staircase curling down the side of the building toward a basement door where all light died. "You will go down those stairs and through that door. Ask for a man named Pasha Morozov. Tell him that you need the information on the final two targets for Gojiba."

"Why me?"

"Because all this is your fault. If you had not gotten rid of the BlackBerry, we would already be on our way."

"And you'd be happily killing people again."

"You are never going to stop me from achieving my goal, Perry. You ought to know that by now. Do you wish to know the definition of a tragic hero?"

"Not particularly."

"A tragic hero is an individual who, with every attempt to restore things to normal, only pushes himself further away from normalcy." She nodded. "That is you, Perry."

"Great," I said, and sighed. "At least you were paying attention in English Lit."

"Yes."

"Who is this Morozov guy anyway?"

"Surveillance specialist. A source of information."

"He's the guy who wiretapped our house for you?"

"Through a third party, yes. I do not speak directly to anyone. He does not know me."

"And he's just supposed to give me this information?"

"You may need to persuade him."

"Maybe you better come along," I said. "You know, just in case there's some misunderstanding."

"Don't worry." The corners of her mouth dimpled slightly. "I believe that he will recognize you."

"Why? Why would he recognize me? Wait—why are you smiling?"

"Because you are an idiot," she said. "Is this how you wish to gamble with your family's lives, standing out here arguing a point that you cannot win?"

"You realize if I die in there, then neither of us gets what we want."

Gobi nodded sagely. "Then do not die."

Taking in a breath, I started walking toward the building, approaching the staircase, and stopped. Down in the shadows just outside the door, something glimmered, a belt buckle or some metallic object flickering off the ambient light. It made me think of the fairy-tale troll that lived under the bridge, and I hesitated, feeling its eye upon me.

"I need to talk to Pasha."

The shadow-troll slithered into the light and revealed himself to be a hulking giant in a shiny red tracksuit with the sleeves shoved up to the elbow, exposing muscle-corded forearms that looked to be built out of dozens of clenched fists. His face was the biggest fist of all, with a knuckle for the nose and two cheap signet rings for eyes.

"Pasha Morozov," I said. "Is he in there?"

"No."

I glanced back at the street, but Gobi was gone.

"I need to speak to him. It's important. Please."

The guard had already started to slink back into the shadow.

"Tell him it's about Gobija Zaksauskas."

The guard froze and then reemerged, a scowl imprinted over the lower half of his face like a poorly healed incision. A moment later a door scraped open, throwing a wedge of dim light across the corrugated metal stairs. A murmur of faint cries and something else came from inside—a thick-throated snarling sound from the depths of the building, as if the darkness itself were fighting for its life. It started like a howl and ended with a high whinnying shriek, then fell silent.

The door clanked shut.

I looked at the stairs.

The door opened again and the guard stepped out.

"This way."

"Ah . . ." I said, "you know, actually, is there any way maybe he could come out here and talk to me?"

"No."

Inside, the howling snarl rose up a second time. "What's going on in there?" I asked. "Are you breeding wolves or something?"

The guard's expression didn't change. "Come, if you are coming. Otherwise—"

"Okay, all right." I stepped down the stairs, trying not to lose my footing, then went inside. A dirty, feral odor was wafting out. It reminded me of the Humane Society Animal Shelter in New Haven, where we'd once gone to adopt a cat for Annie's birthday, choosing from a hundred yowling, miserable animals. The smell of sawdust and ammonia stung my sinuses and made my eyes water. From inside I heard men's voices now, coming from somewhere in front of me.

The hallway was dark, the damp concrete floor cracked and uneven, the ceiling low enough that I had to stoop forward to keep from hitting my head. Twenty yards ahead, a room blazed with light. The men's voices rang out louder, cheering and shouting in another language—Russian, probably—and the slobbering, snarling, wild night noise burst up again, shaking the air around me. I felt my kidneys go loose, and my legs trembled once before seeming to disappear at the knees. I tried to think of anything I could do to avoid going any farther and instead heard the cold voice of dispassionate logic in the back of my mind.

*Think of Annie and your family. If you don't do this, they're dead.*

*Gobi wouldn't really—*

*She might.*

I took another step.

The room was packed with heavy, hard-looking men in shirtsleeves and suspenders, twenty or thirty of them, gathered around a pit that had been dug directly into the floor. They were all shouting and waving their arms, pumping cash-stuffed fists in the air. An empty cage stood off to one side, its door open. Edging closer, I saw something huge and black tied to a stake in the middle of the pit, jerking and snarling in its harness. It looked too big and round to be a dog.

After a second I realized it was a bear.

Two dogs—pit bulls, or some kind of half-breed variant of them—were in the pit with it, lunging and snapping at the bear while it swiped at them with its claws. The men surrounding the pit cheered louder. The primitive expressions on their faces made what was going on in the pit look positively sophisticated by comparison. Their cheering overwhelmed the roar of the bear. None of the men noticed that I was even there.

Then I saw Morozov.

I figured it must have been him because he was the only one who seemed completely disinterested in the bear-fight.

He slouched in the corner with his back to me, a sallow scarecrow lost in the folds of an oversize suit. Plasma TV screens, monitors, and electronics equipment surrounded him like a glowing blue nest, bathing his skin in a pale light that made him look like he might have suffered from some blood-borne disease in childhood from which he'd never fully recovered. A massive pair of headphones rested over his head.

I tapped him on the shoulder. "Pasha?" I asked, figuring we might as well start right off on a first-name basis.

He turned around slowly, showing me sunken eyes that never seemed to stop moving, and slipped off the headphones. Behind us, the bear gave a great, bellowing roar and I heard one of the dogs give a shrill yip of pain. The cheering rose up again.

"What is it?" he asked.

"My name is Perry Sto—"

His fist came down on the table hard enough to make the equipment shake. His expression did not change.

"That is not what I asked."

"I'm looking for information," I said. "I'm here with Gobija Zaksauskas."

"Impossible."

"Why?"

"Because." He glanced disinterestedly back at the room, and then at me. "Gobija Zaksauskas is dead."

# 21

"What?" I was sure that I'd misheard him over the noise of the fight. "I didn't—"

"Are you deaf *and* stupid?" Morozov asked. "She's dead. They beat her and cut her throat right here in Brooklyn."

"Who did?"

He gazed at me until I realized that he wasn't going to answer.

"When was this?"

"Three years ago."

"That's . . ." I shook my head. "Maybe it was a different Gobija?"

Morozov simply stared at me. He seemed to be trying to decide if I was worth getting up for or if it would be easier just to toss me in the pit with the bear and the dogs. In the end he settled on a dusting-off gesture with one hand.

"Get the hell out of here."

"Wait—"

But someone had already grabbed my arms, snapping me backwards. Morozov returned his attention to his screens. He picked up a bottle of vodka from the desk in front of him and refilled a glass, tossing in a handful of blueberries from a ceramic bowl and swirling them around.

"I need the information for the last two hits tonight."

Morozov stopped what he was doing and made a slight chin gesture to whoever was behind me. Abruptly, my arms flew loose. At the same moment there was another shriek from the dogs and a huge cheer from the crowd of men as money changed hands. The fight was over.

"What did you say?" Morozov asked.

"The information on the last two hits. I lost it. I need it back."

"*You?*"

"I'm the guy. You know . . . the killer."

"You."

"The assassin, yeah."

Morozov burst out laughing without seeming to move his face. It was achieved through a nostril twitch and a slight shift of the shoulders.

"You must have heard about what happened to Milos tonight at Harry Cipriani's?" I asked. "I was the one that stabbed him. Blood spurted out of his mouth like a fountain. They had to carry him out in a bucket. And those hits at the 40/40 Club and downtown in the Financial District."

"That . . . was you?"

"Yes."

He pushed back his chair and took a longer look at me in my tattered, bloody tuxedo. "What did you use to kill the old man?"

"A butterfly knife."

"Like this one?" Morozov reached into his jacket and flipped open a short, sharp blade, laying it on the table next to his cigarettes. "Show me."

I stared into his eyes. I thought about my father, and every other tin-pot tyrant who had ever sat behind a desk or a table and demanded that I somehow prove myself. I thought about how much I'd already lost, and what I had yet to lose. Given the night, it didn't seem like much.

"Why do you have to be such a dick about it?" I asked.

Morozov raised his eyebrows, mouth tightening by degrees. "What?"

"Look, I need information," I said, gesturing at the screens and keyboards. "And you've obviously got it. If that's a problem . . ." My mind flashed to the name that Gobi had used when we were in the Jaguar. ". . . maybe we should talk to Santamaria about it together."

Morozov glanced up. "Santamaria?"

"That's right . . . Santamaria. Who do you think has guys tailing me here? Santamaria's been up my ass all night. You think I *like* coming out to Red Hook at midnight on a Saturday night? I ditched the information on the last two targets on my way here—"

"You?" He tapped my chest with one crooked finger. "You know Santamaria?"

"That's what I'm saying."

"And you're sure it's Santamaria's people following you?"

"Two heavily armed ex-military douchebags in a black Humvee," I said. "You do the math."

"Could be anyone."

"You want to take that chance?"

Morozov didn't answer. He finished his cigarette and dropped it to the floor, ground it under his heel. In the background I heard

108

men shouting at the bear and the bear growling back at them. Morozov scratched one grubby-nailed finger over his cheek, letting the moment stretch, until I tugged up my sleeve and looked at where my watch would be if I'd been wearing one.

"I don't have all night," I said. "Are you going to give me the information or not?"

Without answering, he turned back to one of the keyboards and typed in a command. A second later, the screen above his head flipped to a new image, showing an empty kitchen.

"Wait a second," I said. "Is that my *house?*"

"This footage is two months old." Morozov punched another key. The screen switched to the second-floor hallway as seen from above. I saw a pile of laundry outside my bedroom door. The door opened and I saw myself walk out in a pair of boxer shorts. I picked up a pair of socks from the top of the laundry and sniffed them, then put them on.

"Why are you taping my house?"

Morozov blinked. "You paid me to."

"Me?"

"You are the assassin, are you not?"

"Well, yeah." On the monitor screen I watched myself go up to a mirror in the hallway and lean in to squeeze a zit. I remembered that zit. It had sprouted on the tip of my nose for two weeks and seemed never to go away. It had just sat there throbbing like a tiny, angry heart.

"Fascinating," Morozov said. "An assassin with pimples."

"Look . . . do you have the information on the last two hits or not?"

He tapped another series of keys. The footage of my house disappeared and was replaced by columns of text. Clicking down, he hit a button. A second later, two sheets of paper spooled out of the laser printer next to his feet.

"Thanks." I reached out for the papers and he grabbed my wrist.

"What is this?"

I looked down where he was already staring at the words stamped on the back of my hand.

UNDERAGE.

"Part of my cover," I said. "It was—"

He didn't release my hand. "What was the name of the first man you killed?"

"Now you want to test me?"

"I do." Now he was grinning, right into my face, close enough that I could smell his eyeballs. "I have decided that I *do* want to test you. The first man you killed tonight at the 40/40 Club. What was his name?"

Before I could answer, he slammed my hand down on the table, his other hand picking up the butterfly knife. He looked down at my fingers.

"Now. How many lies have you told me?"

I licked my lips. "Listen . . ."

"Four? Five?" He nodded. "Five at least, I think. Little ones. So we'll start with the pinky."

# 22

What are the responsibilities of an educated person? (Yale)

The scream that came from the other side of the room sounded like no other sound I'd ever heard. That was because it was actually several screams at once—human and animal mixed together. When Morozov heard it he dropped the knife and let my hand go at the same time. He jumped up, his elbow knocking over the bottle. Vodka went spilling down the side of the keyboard, pooling around a bundle of cables, sparking off the wires.

I looked back. A man was running toward me with an enormous bleeding gash in his upper arm. I could see the shoulder joint through his torn flesh. Behind him, men ran in every direction. I heard furniture tipping over. A Tiffany lamp went sideways with a splintering clink.

Then I saw the bear.

It had gotten loose from the pit and was crashing across the room, still trailing its harness, mauling people as it went. Nobody seemed able to find the exit. I saw a man pull out a pistol and try to shoot at it, and the bear lunged, landing on top of him with its front paws and burying its snout in the man's face. I heard the shots going off, very loud in the enclosed space, and the man's screams became different, soggy and thin and then gone.

The bear sat up, its muzzle dripping red, and let out a chest-shaking roar. Across the room another man stood up from behind a bar with a machine gun. He started shooting. An ellipsis of bullet holes appeared in the wall above my head. The bear howled and pounced. I heard glass explode in front of me.

I ran for the door.


"You're dead," I said.

Gobi didn't answer. We were sitting in a dive bar on Van Brunt Street, six blocks away from the red brick building. It was one thirty in the morning, but the place was still full enough to offer some semblance of urban camouflage. Hipsters and longshoremen and a few lost-looking Manhattanites were sitting on the couches and mismatched chairs that filled the back half of the room. Nobody seemed to notice the kid in the tuxedo and the dark-haired girl in the dress hunched together in the corner over a burning red candle.

"Did you hear what I just said?" I asked.

"Be silent." Gobi flattened the bloodstained pages that I'd gotten from Morozov across the wooden table in front of her, concentrating on what was printed there.

"Morozov said you died three years ago. He said somebody cut your throat. That's why the old man freaked out when you told him your name, right? He was looking at a ghost."

"Lower your voice."

"What's going on here?"

She drew in a breath and looked up at me. "Why does it matter?"

"What?"

"All you want to do is survive the night. Get away from me and never see me again. What does it matter to you what I am?"

"Because—" I didn't know how to finish.

"Believe me, Perry. The less that you know about me, the better."

"Yeah," I said. "I used to think that too. But now I'm thinking knowledge is power."

"Then you are wrong."

"What really happened to Gobija Zaksauskas?"

"You are looking at her."

"I don't believe in spooks," I said, amazed at how much effort it took to get those words out. Even after all we'd been through, I half expected her to give me a look like I'd gone crazy, or even laugh in my face.

But she didn't do either of those things. Instead she reached across the table and took my hand, placing it on the side of her neck alongside the scar so that I could feel her pulse. Her skin was soft and pliant, almost hot to the touch. I could feel the blood tracing through her veins and felt her eyes on mine. It was like she saw something in me that I didn't see, wouldn't see for a long time.

"Does this feel like a ghost to you?"

"Why are you doing this?"

"Doing what?"

I pulled my hand away. "There's nobody watching. You don't have to put on an act."

"What is wrong, Perry? You do not like the way I feel?"

I rolled my eyes. "Give me a break."

"Admit it. This is your fantasy."

"*What?*"

She brought out a tube of red lipstick and rolled it slowly over

113

her lips. "Ever since you first found out you were getting a female foreign exchange student living in your house you dreamed of a girl in thigh-high stockings who would seduce you, show you things you never knew before, and when she left, whisper '*Au revoir,* Perry' . . . even if she were not French."

"Except with you it's more like *Hasta la vista,* baby."

"But true, no?"

"*No.*"

"Then tell me the truth," she said.

"The truth? The truth is that right now my life as I know it is basically finished. I'm an accomplice to murder three times over. I might as well just go turn myself in to the cops now, throw myself on the mercy of the court. Maybe I can get my diploma in prison. Lots of guys get their law degree in the joint. I bet there's even a special program I can apply for."

"Perry."

"My dad could put in a good word with the warden. If I just watch myself in the showers—"

"*Perry.*"

"What?"

"I asked you to lower your voice."

"Why?" I said, getting louder. "What are you going to do, shoot me?" People at the nearby couches and tables were starting to look up. "Are you gonna—"

*Whap!* Her fist cracked me across the jaw. The world erupted in dozens of tiny flashbulbs pulsing on and off throughout my skull, and I stumbled backwards, off-balance, shook it off—and I lunged at her, tripping over a chair leg before I even came within striking distance. "You bitch!"

Gobi grabbed me and swung me around, straight-arming me into a shelf of pottery. Little glazed teapots and cups and bowls tinkled to the floor around my feet. The group of pseudohipsters at the sofa behind us gathered their drinks and took a few steps back, getting out their cell phones either to call the cops or snap pictures.

"Now," Gobi said, gripping my collar, "you and I—"

I pumped my arms out and shoved her back as hard as I could. I wasn't particularly strong, but she was light and tumbled farther than I'd thought before colliding with a tray of drinks behind her. Rising up, soaked in booze, Gobi lifted the tray and flung it at me.

I ducked it—my reflexes were still decent—and ran straight at her. Gobi scowled as if she couldn't believe that I was coming back for more, but if there was one thing I'd learned from competitive swimming, it was endurance. As she cocked back her fist and prepared to administer the deathblow, my foot slipped on the wet floor and I went flying, landing hard on top of her with my face between her legs.

"Hey, dirtbag," some guy shouted. "What kind of animal beats up a woman?"

"*Shut up,*" Gobi and I both shouted at the same time, and she took the opportunity to grab me by the ears, pluck my head out of her crotch, and bounce it off the floor. I saw red and tasted white pine, sat up, and pounced on top of her, delivering at least one punch that might have connected, although my knuckles were roast beef. We both staggered to our feet, circling each other warily.

"Just tell me one thing," I said. "One thing you never lied about."

She blew a strand of hair from her face. "Do you remember the time that you helped me with math class?"

"What, you mean that Stock Exchange PowerPoint presentation?"

"Yes. You assisted me."

"Assisted you? I did the whole thing for you the morning that it was due."

Gobi smiled. "I had been in the city all night setting up a weapons buy in the Bronx. I snuck in just before dawn. You saved my life that day."

"So you lied about that too."

"I am telling you the truth *now,*" she said.

I licked a drop of blood from my swelling upper lip. "What about the day you stayed home sick from school, right before Thanksgiving? Did you really have food poisoning?"

"Why, did you suspect something?"

"Well, I wondered why you smelled like WD-40 at the dinner table."

She raised her eyebrows, her smile widening. "You caught on to that, did you?"

"You still had a grease streak right across your eyebrow."

"That was elevator cable lubricant. I had to repel down the maintenance shaft of that building in the Financial District to crack the security system. How do you think I got in there tonight?"

"You know, my sister heard you calling somebody about buying guns one night."

"Annie is a wonderful girl," Gobi said. "She reminds me of . . ."

"Who?"

She hesitated and shook her head. "No one. You are fortunate to have such a wonderful sister."

"Which is why you planted a bomb in our basement?"

"How many times do you wish for me to say sorry?"

"I should have shot you when I had the chance."

Gobi laughed. "Too little, too late."

"I'm serious. I—"

She swung at me. I took ahold of her throat, spinning and losing my balance. The door bumped open and we spilled out onto the sidewalk.

After landing hard on the concrete, I started to get to my feet, and Gobi grabbed me, pulling me back down on top of her. I jerked myself free, stole a quick breath, and tried to get upright before she could get another punch in.

She leaned up and kissed me. Her mouth tasted like lipstick, blood, and gunpowder. It was also the softest thing that I'd ever felt, and in spite of the pain I felt my mouth opening so that my tongue could flick out to taste hers. The heat came off her face like a furnace. Our tongues moved around each other's, swirling and dueling. Finally she broke the kiss. It was like surfacing after a long, intoxicating dive through a sea of Red Bull.

"What was that for?" I managed.

"I am beginning to like you, Perry."

I shivered out a breath. "You've got a kooky way of showing it."

"Have you ever felt more alive?"

"Once or twice, yes."

Gobi was still looking at me, lips half parted, eyes searching the depths of whatever was inside me. She looked lost and young and totally uncontrolled, a reflection of how I felt now, in a place that I'd never been before, somewhere that nobody would ever think to look for me. I had the sudden, ridiculous, absolutely compelling vision of chucking everything—school, music, my family and friends—and running away with her, away from the rest of the world.

I figured we'd last about a week.

"Are you all right?" she asked.

"My head hurts."

"Is the lipstick," she smiled. "There is a mind-control drug in it. You are now completely under my power."

"Uh-huh."

"Kiss me again."

I didn't move. "Somebody sold you some faulty goods."

"The drug is slow-acting but very potent." She leaned forward again, whispering, just brushing her mouth against mine. "By dawn you will be mine."

"Just promise me you won't hurt my family."

She went serious. "Families get hurt, Perry. There are no guarantees this side of the grave."

"You're a real bitch, you know that?"

"I never denied it."

I swung at her. She caught my fist.

"Too slow."

I let myself tilt forward just enough for our foreheads to touch, then reached for her neck and put my fingers on the scar, tracing the thin curve of raised tissue.

"What happened there?"

Her gaze shifted away. "A painful memory."

"Like what, getting your throat cut and coming back from the grave?"

Gobi straightened up. The mood didn't just break—it shattered into a million sharp and spiky pieces that lay all over the sidewalk like dragon's teeth.

Then she shuddered and fell still.

"Gobi?"

She leaned forward again, and I caught her. For a moment we just stood there together in front of the dive bar, and when I felt her

118

legs starting to give way, I lowered her back down the front steps. A couple of people came out the front door and walked around us, staring at us but not saying anything.

A few seconds later, Gobi raised her head, her eyes foggy but already starting to clear.

"Perry?"

I nodded. "I'm here."

"We have to go," she said. "We have to . . . get a car."

"Maybe we should just wait here a second."

"No, now." She didn't look at me. "It's time to finish this."

# 23

If you were to look back on your high school years, what advice would you give someone beginning his or her high school career? (Simmons)

A half-hour later we were rolling down East Eighty-Fifth Street in a stolen BMW F10, which I could only presume was Gobi's idea of keeping a low profile. It had taken her less than two minutes to crack the steering column, disable the antitheft system, and hotwire the ignition, using only a pair of wire cutters and a screwdriver that she'd found in the trunk. Whoever owned the car had terrible taste in music, and Michael Bublé serenaded us on the sound system, doing his best to cheer us up. It wasn't working.

"The Upper East Side," I said.

"Stop up here."

I pulled up in front of a fire hydrant, removed the screwdriver that she'd jammed into the ignition, and allowed the engine to shudder to a halt. We got out and stood in the middle of the silent street, eyeing the disapproving rows of residential brownstones on either side of us.

"That's the one," she pointed. "Right there."

I hesitated. The massive four-story building towering overhead had tall, rounded windows and black double doors protected by wrought-iron curlicues that looked as though they could deflect a missile attack. It was a fortress for someone very dangerous and rich, where they could pretend to be civilized. Ivy rippled across its brick face, thick and out of control, smothering the surfaces. It made the building look diseased, as if it had some kind of architectural gangrene.

In the glow from the streetlight I saw Gobi loading bullets into a clip and sticking the gun into her dress. She reached down into her boot and flicked out a straight razor, inspecting the blade, and slipped it away again.

"Come on," she said. "Time to go to work."

"Nope."

"Excuse me?"

"I'm not helping you kill anybody else. It's just not happening. I'm done."

"What makes you think you have a choice?"

"You know why? I'll tell you. Because we were just kissing in the street, and deep down, I don't believe you could actually blow up my house or kill my sister. I just don't, and she's probably not even in the house anymore anyway, so if you want to go in there and shoot somebody, fine, but you're on your own."

Gobi paused, seeming to consider all of this. "What is it that you want to hear from me, Perry? Do you want me to tell you that these are bad people that I am killing tonight? Because they are. They are *very* bad people. They deserve to die, each and every one of them."

"Nobody *deserves* to die."

"Oh, really?"

"Okay, I mean, maybe people like Hitler and Pol Pot . . . dictators, tyrants, African warlords who starve their people into submission . . . but that guy at the bar wasn't an evil man."

"How do you know? Because he had drinks with Hemingway?"

"I just know."

A car appeared at the end of the street, cruising slowly by. We both froze and watched it pass.

"It is not safe out here."

"And it's safer in there?"

"It is safer with me."

"Forget it," I said. "I'm still not going in."

"Then you are being very stupid."

"I got twenty-two hundred on my SATs," I said. "How stupid is that?"

"Stupid enough not to realize when someone cares about you."

"Meaning what, exactly?"

She looked at me.

"What do you think it means?"

Footsteps scuffed up the sidewalk behind us. I heard voices, two of them, the low, self-conscious murmurs of men who were used to being quiet. Gobi grabbed me and yanked me into the shadows.

A second later I leaned back out. Up the street I saw two men walking toward the BMW. One wore khakis and a barn coat. The other was dressed in a leather jacket, and I didn't need to see the teardrop tattoo on his cheek to know who they were.

"Shit," I whispered, "it's those thugs from downtown. What do we do?"

Not waiting for me, she seized my arm and pulled me up to the front steps of the brownstone, keeping our backs to the sidewalk while she rapped on the door. Seconds later, I heard latches scraping and the door opened. A very tall, extremely glamorous hostess in a formal gown and five-inch lashes was standing there with a martini in her hand. The liquor made her smile look like it had been put on sideways. "Well, *hello.*"

"Hello," Gobi said. "I hope we're not too late for the party."

"Don't be ridiculous, darling," the hostess giggled, tossing her long blond hair. "It's *early.*" Over her shoulder, I saw clusters of people dancing and drinking, their faces barely visible in little pools of dim light. "Come inside."

The hostess disappeared immediately after letting us through the door. The air was smoky, dense with perfume and the smell of sour wine breath. Gobi and I moved through a marble entryway with a high ceiling and a crystal chandelier. Oil paintings, glass sculptures, and doorways funneled down into a formal sitting room and lavishly appointed dining area, all filled with people talking over the thump of urban hip-hop. From one of the back rooms I heard a woman scream with laughter while a man's voice said, "Nope, nope, nope . . . never in a million years . . ."

Party guests, the very rich and their friends, had broken off into special little subcommittees of twos and threes. I saw a couple kissing on a Persian rug next to a coffee table full of red plastic cups, having reached a moment of perfect invisibility. Nobody cared that they were there. The party had reached the point at which the rules weren't in effect anymore.

Gobi gestured at the staircase in front of us. The message was clear: *We're going up.*

"Forget it," I said. "I'm staying here."

"Fair enough." She glanced out at the street. "Bring the car around."

"I can't."

"Why not?"

"You hot-wired it, remember?"

"So this time, you do it."

"I don't know how."

"Weren't you paying attention?"

"Yeah," I said, "but I'm not a car thief any more than you're a foreign exchange student who wrote that PowerPoint about the New York Stock Exchange."

She flicked her eyes up and to the left, where we're taught people normally look while accessing memory. "The New York Stock Exchange is located at Eleven Wall Street. It is the world's largest stock exchange by market capitalization of its listed companies at two point eight trillion dollars. Shall I continue?"

"Nobody likes a smart aleck."

"I was paying attention, Perry," she said. "Weren't you?"

# 24

Attach a small photograph of something important to you and explain its significance. (Stanford)

After slipping back through the front door, I stood for a moment perfectly still on the front steps of the brownstone, checking out Eighty-Fifth Street. There was no sign of anyone else around. Except for the faint rumble of the music behind me, the world was very quiet, still enough that I could hear the slow tidal pull and release of my breath.

Something scurried across the street—a rat, I thought—and disappeared between some trash cans.

Gradually I descended the steps, careful to keep my footsteps silent. There was no sign of the two guys I'd seen earlier. The BMW sat where we had left it, in front of the fire hydrant. I wasn't sure that I could get the engine hot-wired again, but I *had* watched what Gobi did the first time and thought I might be able to pull it off. That was ridiculous, of course, but my mind got as far as Gobi and just sort of stopped.

I crept up to the BMW, opened the driver's side door, and lowered myself in behind the wheel. The screwdriver that I'd pulled from the steering column was nowhere to be found.

I looked over at Gobi's bag, slumped in the passenger seat like some silent third party that had followed us dutifully through the night. Reaching inside, my hand passed over piles of clothing, boxes of ammunition, two knives, a leather shoulder harness, and a manila envelope.

I took the envelope out and opened it.

A picture fell out and onto my lap.

I picked it up and looked at it.

The photo was old and faded, creased down the middle, as if it had been folded and unfolded hundreds of times, shoved down at the bottom of suitcases, and buried in pockets. It showed two little girls in long, dark dresses, standing next to a tree in front of a modest one-story house. I guessed they were about six or seven years old. The sky behind them was a peculiar shade of greenish gray.

Both girls wore their hair pinned up away from their forehead in the stark, severe style that I recognized from Gobi's days as a foreign exchange student at Upper Thayer. One of the girls clutched a doll; the other was cradling a small, slightly annoyed-looking tortoiseshell cat, its tail dangling from the girl's arms. A small round table stood on the lawn in front of them, set up with teacups, saucers, spoons, napkins, and a teapot. Both of them were smiling shyly, as if whoever took the picture had surprised them in the middle of their favorite game.

My conscious mind absorbed what my instincts had already realized: one of the girls was Gobi; the other was so similar that she could have been her twin. I couldn't exactly say how I knew which was which; some nuance of the smile, a subtle glint of humor that the other, more earnest girl didn't reveal.

I held the photo directly up to my eyes, looking more closely.

Both girls were wearing pendants around their necks.

Half-hearts.

*I am Death.*

That was when the two men sat up from the back seat.


"Good night, sweetheart," the one with the teardrop tattoo said, opening his jacket, and I saw the sawed-off shotgun emerge from under his arm just before he swung the barrel over the seat, cracking me across the bridge of my nose. I felt myself sinking down, one more square peg pounded into the round hole of oblivion.

# 25

Where do you see yourself in ten years? (Rutgers)

A dripping sound awakened me, the echoing subterranean *plip-plop* of water forming puddles in some underground space.

The next thing I noticed was the pain.

It started in my nose. I couldn't breathe. My throat and sinuses felt plugged up, waxed shut with hunks of clotted blood. Pain throbbed through my facial bones and ran down my neck, branching into my arms and wrists.

My hands were tied behind me. Turning my head slowly, I saw that I was in a metal folding chair in some kind of dimly lit industrial basement. Although I couldn't see more than twenty yards in any given direction, I could make out vague shapes of exposed pipes and light fixtures overhead, and the dripping sound was coming from somewhere beyond that, from some piece of leaky plumbing recessed into the crossbeams and cobwebs. It was cold and damp down here, the gray space receding far back into a series of smaller warrens and alcoves. Rusty lengths of chain and rope dangled from the pipes over my head. Some of the chains had meathooks hanging off the ends of them.

I heard a sound and looked over.

The sound came again, a grating, scratching noise. Twenty feet of exposed gray concrete in front of me, Gobi sat tied to her own chair.

Whatever the two guys outside had done to me, they had done much worse to her. Her lips were swollen and split open. Her entire right eye had puffed shut, leaving only a thin, downward-slanting slit with a pupil glinting moist and terribly aware. A long razor slash crisscrossed her left cheek down to her chin, and when she opened her mouth, I saw that one of her front teeth had been knocked out.

She was staring down, murmuring to herself in Lithuanian.

"Gobi?"

She didn't answer.

"Gobi?"

She tilted her head and looked at me with her one good eye.

"Where are we?"

She cocked her head, listening. From somewhere above us, we heard faint voices and the squeak of floorboards as boots thudded overhead, stopped, and moved on.

"Where did those guys take us?"

She shook her head for silence. The footsteps crossed above us again and I heard another voice, a woman, but I couldn't make out what was being said. The pain was making me breathe more heavily, and the air whistling through my nose blocked out most of the sound. I tried to dredge up details from after Teardrop Tattoo had smashed me in the face with the shotgun barrel, but everything after that was a tremulous, blood-soaked blur. I vaguely remembered begging whoever it was to stop, and the sound of their laughter, growing fainter.

My eyes had fully adjusted to the darkness now.

That was when I saw the cages.

They looked like kennels for big dogs, except with thicker bars and padlocks dangling open from their latches. The ones that I saw from here were all empty except for stained newspaper on the bottom and balled-up scraps of something that might have been rags. It reminded me of the Russian's operation in Brooklyn, and I wondered if we'd somehow ended up back there again.

"They are for people," Gobi whispered.

"What?"

"The cages."

I stared. "They put people in those things?"

Gobi tilted her head upward at the indistinct voices and footsteps. Then came a sound like someone dropping a series of increasingly heavy wooden blocks down the stairs. A moment later, a bright oval of high-powered light swung across the walls around me, carving out exaggerated shadows of imaginary objects—a vulture, a wolf's head, the serrated teeth of a bear trap. One by one they disappeared.

The footsteps slowed, approaching. The man behind the flashlight plodded in front of me and stopped, pouring light directly into Gobi's face. He was wearing a long cattleman's coat that went almost down to his ankles, and the collar was flipped up so that the only part of him that I could actually see was the apex of his wide bald head. It was covered with stiff little tufts of hair like bristles on a boar's snout.

"Gobija Zaksauskas," he said in a heavy accent that could have been eastern European, Russian, or some other combination. I realized he was holding something in his hand, some sort of ID. "That is you?"

She nodded and muttered back in Lithuanian.

"These papers are forgeries," the man said. "What is your real name?"

"Tatiana Kazlauskieni."

"I'll ask you again. What is your name?"

"Amelia Earhart."

"Lying pig," the man said. "You think this is funny?"

"I think it is hilarious."

"I will show you funny."

He stepped in front of Gobi, blocking my view of her, and did something fast and brutal with his hand. There was a slap and a hollow thump, and Gobi coughed with pain.

"Now," the man said, "what is your name?"

"The Virgin Mary."

"Who trained you?"

"The Holy Spirit."

Another clank and a thump, and this time Gobi cried out loud.

"You asshole!" I shouted. "Leave her alone!"

The man was making little grunting noises down in his chest cavity, as if breathing cost him effort. "I think we have a cage for you down here somewhere," he said. "For your friend too"—the flashlight beam pivoted around and hit my face, momentarily blinding me—"although he might not be worth keeping."

"He has nothing to do with this," Gobi said.

The man turned back to her, dragging a chain across the bare floor. "Did you speak to me, gypsy trash?"

"I said—"

*Whack!* The hand clapped down and slammed into her with full force. Again I didn't see where it actually made contact, but it must have hurt even more, because Gobi let out a sharp cry.

"You will speak when spoken to." The man's tone had changed again. Now it was brisk and didactic, like that of an obedience instructor training an obstinant dog, and I hated him for it, the hate momentarily eclipsing all fear and reason. "Do you understand?"

"It is not complicated," Gobi said.

"You have been very stupid tonight," the man told her. "Did you not think we would be ready for you when you came?"

Gobi said nothing, just maintained eye contact, chin tilted defiantly upward.

"Who sent you?"

She didn't move.

"I asked you a question." The hand swung up again, dangling the chain this time, and I saw him run it slowly over her face, streaking the blood that trickled from her nostrils, smearing it upward into her hair. "Where did you get your information?"

No answer from Gobi. I cleared my throat.

"Listen," I said. "Sir."

The man lumbered back around to look at me. This time he kept the flashlight trained low, allowing me my first real look at him. The face was bulbous and pink and hairless, utterly unremarkable, a Sunday school teacher's face, and that was the most unsettling part of it. Although he was probably my dad's age or older, the slack, anonymous complexion and dead eyes made it impossible to exactly pinpoint his age. He could have been a wax statue, a young actor made up to look old, or an amateurishly embalmed corpse.

"My father is an attorney," I said. "If he knew I was here, I know he'd pay you whatever you wanted to let us go. If you just let me call him, I'm sure we can get this all worked out."

The dead-eyed man regarded me without the slightest change of expression. I could hear the links of the chain jangling softly in his hand.

*He's going to hit me,* I thought. *Like he hit Gobi. He's going to smash my face in with the chain.*

But he turned away again. It was as if he'd heard some noise from this corner of the basement but couldn't see anything there.

"Who sent you here?" he asked Gobi.

"I came on my own," Gobi said.

"Who trained you?"

Gobi said something in Lithuanian, then leaned forward and spat in his face.

The man went straight and very still. I felt myself getting ready to beg for Gobi's life. I would promise whatever I had to, to keep him from killing us.

The man just lowered the chain again. With a sigh, he wiped his face, turned, and went back upstairs.


"Hey." I looked at Gobi. "Are you okay?"

It was a stupid question, but I couldn't think of how else to open the conversation between us. I didn't even think she was going to respond. But after a moment she raised her head and looked at me. Holding my breath, I could hear her feet scraping in the wet shadows.

"I want you to listen to me very carefully, Perry." Her voice was low and intense. "Are you listening?"

"Yes."

"That man's name is Slavin."

"You actually know him?"

"Only by reputation. In a moment he's going to come back downstairs. And he's going to start torturing me."

"What do you call what he's been doing so far?"

"Nothing. Child's play."

"What's he going to do?"

"He will probably begin by ripping my fingernails out. I want you to be ready."

"For what?"

"If you see your chance to run, take it. Do not look back."

"I'm supposed to leave you getting your nails pulled out?"

"Or my teeth," she said. "They are his specialty. Rumor has it that he used to be a dentist in Romania. Now he makes a living doing interrogation for hire."

"Why don't you just tell him what he wants to know?"

"I do not like bullies. And I have never responded well to threats of force." She paused. "Also, I believe he will kill me anyway."

"Why?"

"Because that is what he does."

We sat there in silence, listening to water drip from the pipes into the puddles on the floor. I wondered how badly hurt she really was, if she'd ever let on to it.

"Did you get that guy back on Eighty-Fifth Street?" I asked.

She nodded. "And then I came back out to the car. You were already unconscious. The two men were waiting for me. By the time I saw them, it was too late."

"I'm sorry," I said.

"Why? There was nothing you could do."

"No," I said, "I should have been paying closer attention."

"You did the best you could," she said. "You are not a warrior, Perry, any more than I am a foreign exchange student."

The silence between us felt different now, drawing out and becoming normal, like when you're sleeping outdoors and the other person has stopped talking for a long time, and the only sounds are the noises of the world.

"Gobi—"

"I did not want to tell you any of this," she said very quietly. "But I want to tell you now. So I will tell you the rest of it."

"I saw the picture in your bag," I said. "You and the other girl. She's your sister, isn't she?"

"She was."

"What was her name?"

"Gobija."

"What?"

"She was the first Gobija."

"The one who died?"

Gobi nodded. "Five years ago she and I were backpacking through the Czech Republic together. One night she met a man at a club and went back to his hotel room. I was tired that night and stayed in." Her voice softened slightly, becoming haunted and distant with regret. "If I had just gone with her to the bar, everything might have been different. As it was, she never came back."

"What happened to her?"

"Our state police force was able to find out nothing. Through private channels I began to piece together evidence that she had been brought to America as part of a human trafficking operation. Her captors gave her large doses of heroin until she became dependent on it."

I tried to say something and couldn't.

"Everyone warned me against continuing my investigation," Gobi continued. "They said the people I was going up against were too powerful. I did not care. They said I would die. Again, I did not care. I knew that my life would mean nothing if I did not come back to avenge my sister's honor. But by the time I was able to pinpoint who had taken her here, it was too late. She had died."

I tried to say something, but my throat was too dry. For a second I couldn't even swallow. My chest felt so tight that it ached, and I thought if I didn't say something, or at least try to, I was going to explode.

"Was she the one?" I asked, my voice not even sounding like my own. I tried again. "The one who was killed out in Brooklyn?"

"Yes."

"And you came back under her name," I said. "To settle things."

Gobi let out a breath. "The truth is more complicated than that," she said, "not as neat. But yes. First I had to find weapons and training to do what was needed to punish those who were responsible for what happened."

"Was it that guy Santamaria who did it?"

"Over all others, yes. The man at the 40/40 Club and the one at the building in the financial district and the man on Eighty-Fifth Street, they all played a part in the operation. But it was Santamaria who brought her to Brooklyn and ultimately had her killed. For these people who buy and sell people for money, Santamaria is also the bank, the legitimate means of making dirty money clean. When I found out about that, I spent three years training and equipping myself for this night when all my targets would be in the city at the same time." Her shoulders shuddered. I realized she had begun to cry. The tears ran down her face, trickling in with the blood over the bruises. "My sister was brought to this country as a slave," she said. "She spent the final months of her life being treated like a piece of meat until finally a rich man paid to see a girl get her throat slit. The indignity of such a thing is beyond imagination." She drew in a watery breath. "Unless I took care of it personally, I knew that I would never feel like her honor had been avenged."

"Gobi, I am so sorry."

"It was Santamaria," she said. "The one who ordered the killing."

"What's your real name?" I asked.

"Zusane," she said. "Zusane Zaksauskas. But now I am Gobija, goddess of fire."

"What can I do?" I asked.

"Let me work."

# 26

Write about a group endeavor in which you partici-
pated, and describe your contribution. (Kenyon)

Footsteps thudded down the stairs again, that same unhurried pace
of a workman going about his routine with no particular worry
about the hour. This time Slavin was carrying a toolbox with him.
Laying it in front of Gobi, he squatted down, then popped the
latches and brought out a pair of stainless-steel pliers. I heard keys
jingling, and he reached around behind Gobi's chair. I held my
breath again and heard a lock click open. Slavin leaned forward to
bring Gobi's right hand out in front of her.

"Now you will tell me who you are, and who sent you."

Gobi said something long and elaborate in Lithuanian.

Slavin sighed. "I do not speak that language."

"I said that you should go to hell. I said that your mother will
meet you there and you can lick her ass for all eternity."

Slavin manufactured another laugh, but this one sounded more
stilted, as if he was trying to hold his anger in check, not quite successfully. When he finally responded, his diction was strained and
formal.

"You are very bold," he said, gripping her hand. "We will see how bold you are when I rip your nails out."

"Go ahead," she said. "I feel nothing. I am already dead."

Now Slavin's grin became real again. Real and hungry. "We shall see," he said.

He picked up the pliers. At that same moment, Gobi jerked her knee upward, slamming it into his face. I heard the crack of bone against bone, and Slavin rocked backwards. Gobi's hand dipped into her boot and whipped out the razor. I saw its mirrored surface flash once through the air in front of the man's startled face, and when he staggered backwards clutching his throat, blood was spurting out between his fingers. Slavin tripped over the toolbox and fell into the chains dangling from the pipe, clattering on the floor in a complicated crash of metal and cement and the leather coat. A halo of red pooled behind his head, spreading toward the grate in the floor.

Gobi jumped over him, crossed the distance between us in what looked like three weightless strides, stuck the key in my handcuffs, and twisted it, freeing me.

Without a word, she started up the stairs.

I went after her.

# 27

Who are the people that have done the most to influence your personal development, and in what ways were they influential? (Carleton College)

The door at the top of the stairs was open just a crack.

Through it, over Gobi's shoulder, I could see three people sitting around what looked like a large industrial kitchen walled in by stainless-steel pantries and storage bins. It smelled like old gravy and canned tomato sauce. The only light came from the flat-screen TV on the wall tuned to some low-budget Asian kung fu movie, something from the seventies, full of bad English dubbing and oversaturated color.

In its glow I recognized Teardrop Tattoo and his partner, the resin-haired action figure who looked like he could have been a body double for any number of Hollywood B-actors, sitting at a plain wooden table and smoking cigarettes in grumpy, exhausted silence.

The clock on the wall said two fifteen a.m.

Neither man was talking. Teardrop Tattoo was flipping disinterestedly through a car magazine while his partner watched the movie.

The third person in the room was a bony woman in a short skirt and torn stockings, her greasy no-color hair piled on top of her head, where it had already started spilling out in different directions. She walked past the TV, the smoky blue light illuminating the sharp planes of her face, and I saw that her eyes had the dazed, insomniac glassiness of a long-term drug user or someone who'd been abused so long that she'd ceased to feel anything at all. When she turned to get something out of a cabinet, I noticed a long, poorly executed tattoo of a snake winding its way up her arm to the shoulder, where it became an entirely different animal, something with a wolf's head. I thought about what Gobi had told me about her sister and suddenly felt very tired and hopeless. The woman was hobbling around the table with her back to us, pouring drinks for the men.

I leaned forward, the top step creaking under my foot.

Without looking back, Gobi flattened her palm against my chest and stopped me, but it was already too late. Across the room I saw the woman turn around and glance up right at us, suddenly alert.

She looked at us and screamed something that sounded like *"Chai!"*

The men at the table scrambled to their feet, whirling around, grabbing weapons.

Gobi moved.

I'm not really sure how it happened. One second she was directly in front of me. The next second she was a puff of smoke twenty feet away, grabbing the wrist of Teardrop Tattoo, swinging his arm behind him, and slamming his face down onto the table. Glasses fell. The bottle hit the floor and burst. The woman kept screaming. On the other side of the table the second man already had his gun up and pointed. Gobi whirled Teardrop in front of her like a shield, her hand going into his

141

barn coat and whipping out a short-barreled, one-handed machine gun pointing at the man on the other side of the table.

There was a gigantic crash and the room went white with muzzle-flash.

Gobi dropped Teardrop's body, kicked the table forward, and flipped it on top of the woman's leg, pinning her to the floor. Ignoring her, Gobi bent forward and picked up the sawed-off shotgun where it had landed, and pointed it at the other man. If there were sounds, I didn't hear them: The report from the gunfire shut my ears down. For the next several minutes I existed in a kind of Beethoven's landscape of perfect noiseless space.

Gobi's lips moved. The other man's lips moved. Her lips moved again. The other man shook his head, said something. Gobi glanced down at the floor, grabbed a cell phone, and jammed it in the other man's hand, pointing the machine gun at his head.

The man lifted the phone and dialed.

He talked.

He handed the phone back to Gobi. Nodding, she wrote something down on the back of her hand—numbers and a word, an address.

Then she pointed the gun at his head and pulled the trigger.


With the machine pistol in her right hand and the sawed-off in her left, she gestured me out of the doorway. She was saying something, but it still felt like my ears were stuffed with cotton. It would be another few seconds before her first words reached my eardrums successfully.

I followed her across the room, stepping over the bodies.

"Watch out for the blood," she said.

# 28

Describe how a specific place can be used to illustrate your personality. (Harvard)

"Santamaria is the last," Gobi said.

I was still thinking of her as Gobi, not Zusane, as we limped back out onto the empty sidewalk into the cold night air. New York was still here, but it had changed in our absence. It was long after midnight, and vast walls of fog off the river shimmered along the sidewalks like the ghosts of tenements that had long ago been leveled to make way for the parking garages and office buildings. It was a spectral Manhattan, a double-exposed landscape where the past folded back over on itself in overlapping decades.

"Where are we?"

Her breath made a little whistling sound. "Tenth Avenue."

"I don't even remember getting here." Though it was true, this wasn't even what I meant to say. My true sentiment—that this didn't even remotely resemble the New York that I remembered—made so little sense in the context of the moment that it was snuffed out on the way through my speech center.

"We need to get across town."

Gobi stumbled, falling to her knees and collapsing onto her side. My first thought was that she'd had another petit mal seizure, and then I saw the blood on her chest.

That was when I realized she'd been shot.

I bent down over her, turning her over on the sidewalk as gently as I could, looking at the red-saturated swath of dress under her right breast. The fabric rippled against her skin and I saw the hole where the bullet had punched through the flesh. "We have to get you to a hospital."

She shook her head. "I'm fine."

"No, you're not. You need a doctor."

"Santamaria . . ."

"Forget Santamaria. If your lung collapses you're going to die."

"The bullet is not in my lung."

"How do you know that? Are you a doctor?"

Gobi raised the machine pistol that she'd taken from the men, swung it up, and pointed it at my face. Now her voice was absolutely ironclad. "No."

"Okay, that's just stupid. If you shoot me you'll never make it anywhere."

Gobi arched her neck and twisted her head back, looking behind us, keeping the gun leveled at my head the whole time. "Just . . . help me up. Need . . . a car."

I put my arm around her waist and lifted her up to her feet. She was lighter than I'd expected, even with all her weight resting on me. Up ahead I saw a group of people walking toward us, talking loudly and laughing on their way back from a bar. I draped my tuxedo jacket over her shoulders and drew it across her bloody dress, holding her close as the group passed us. I could feel her breathing against me, irregular and labored. Intense heat poured off her.

"Perry . . ."

"What?"

"Reach inside my stocking." She staggered a little toward an alleyway in front of us, stretched out one hand, and leaned against the wall, then slid the rest of the way to the ground. "Reach in and get it out."

Kneeling down, I slipped my hand up her dress and down the stocking, running my finger along her thigh until I felt a hard round object tucked inside the nylon. Sliding it out, I saw it was a yellow tube: it looked like a highlighter.

"What is it?"

"EpiPen. Adrenaline. You need to inject me with it."

I took the cap off. "Anywhere?"

"In my thigh. Up here."

I uncapped the syringe and stabbed the needle into the flesh of her leg. Gobi winced, stiffened, and then started to relax. The change was unbelievably quick. Her breathing began to normalize, but I still heard the wheezing sound trailing at the end of every breath.

"Better?"

"I will be."

"You still need a doctor."

"And you need a better haircut." Gobi gripped the alley wall and rose unsteadily to her feet. Color had flushed back through her cheeks, and the metallic brightness in her swollen eyes wasn't entirely rational, but it was alive, watchful.

"Santamaria is the only one left." She held up her hand where she'd written the address in ballpoint. "When the job is finished I will go away and be gone forever. The only problem is that this is an office building and I will need clearance to get through security."

I looked at the address: *855 3rd Avenue.*

"There's got to be some mistake." I stared at the writing on her hand. "This is my dad's office."

She looked supremely unsurprised. "Yes?"

"You knew," I said.

Gobi stopped and looked back up at me, her eyes still pumped and twitching with adrenaline. "After everything I went through to put this together, you could not have thought it was just an accident that I chose your family. It was not just random chance."

"But if you already knew, why did you have to call and get the address?"

She drew in a breath and let it leak out from between swollen lips.

"I needed to be sure. At this time of night. Home . . ." She held up her hand. "Or office."

I couldn't speak. I stood there on the corner of Tenth Avenue and Thirtieth Street at three in the morning, mute, mindless, my rented leather shoes nailed to the sidewalk. In the end I was just a stupid rented prince in a stupid prom tuxedo and everything that had happened up until this moment had been a fairy-tale trail of bread crumbs leading through the woods of the night. That I had followed that trail blindly, reacting, responding, somehow thinking that I'd understood what was going on, only made me a bigger idiot than I thought I was before.

"You must realize," Gobi said. "Tonight was all for my sister. For her, I would have done anything." She raised the machine pistol back in my direction. "Anything."

I swallowed. I think I nodded. "What if you're wrong?"

"I am not wrong."

"It's a law office."

"A paragon of innocence."

"Who is it? Who are you going to kill?"

"The one who laundered the money for it. The one who allowed Gobija to be brought here and sold to these animals, exploited and killed for their sport."

"Santamaria."

"Yes."

"Who is it?"

"Give me your card, Perry."

"What?"

"Your key card to get into the office. It is in your wallet behind your driver's license, right in front of the snapshot of you and your sister at Disney World."

"If you knew it was there, why didn't you just take it before now?"

"You would have noticed. You are a smart boy."

A lie, and we both knew it.

She turned and directed her attention up Tenth Avenue, where cabs were running in packs from the last light, headed uptown.

I opened my wallet and took out the magnetic card, handing it to her.

"And now," she said, raising her hand for a cab, "your wish has been granted. You may go home and forget I ever existed." A taxi swung up to the curb. "Whatever happens next is not on your conscience."

"Wait," I said. "Gobi . . ."

She leaned forward, kissing me briefly on the mouth. "*Au revoir*, Perry."

"Wait," I said.

But she didn't.

She climbed into the taxi.

She didn't look back.

# 29

Select three adjectives that describe you and explain. (Bowdoin College)

I didn't have a cell phone. I didn't have a car. I didn't have any cash. I had an ATM card and a calling card and a Visa card that I was allowed to use only in emergencies. Hunched over in the last working public phone in midtown, I punched in the digits. I didn't have to wait long, one ring at the most.

"Hello?"

"Mom?"

"*Perry.*" Relief and exasperation gushed out in equal proportion. "Where are you?"

"I'm still in New York. Mom, listen—"

"Your father and I have been absolutely beside ourselves."

"Where is Dad?"

"He's still in the city looking for you. Are you all right?"

"Mom, listen to me, okay? First, you need to get Annie and get out of the house. It's not safe there."

"Annie already told me about that," she said. "Perry, I don't know what kind of joke you're trying to pull, but this isn't funny. There are limits to publicity."

"What?"

"Your band. I know you're trying to get noticed, but this isn't the way to go about it."

"Mom, it's not about the *band*."

"Oh no? So you were just playing this show tonight for fun?"

"Mom, please, just listen. Take the cell phone and get out of the house now."

"Do you have any idea what time it is, Perry?"

"Yes," I said. "I do. I'm cold and tired and alone and I'm in the middle of New York City in the middle of the night so yes, I do know what time it is. And I need you to get Annie and get out of the house right now, please, okay?"

"Where are you?"

"I told you, I'm—"

"Yes, but where exactly?"

"The corner of Eighth Avenue and Thirty-Third Street," I said, "why?"

Quiet, for a long time.

"I'm calling your father," she said. "Stay where you are."


After I got off the phone with my mom, I stood on the corner in front of a Korean deli, watching the traffic roll by. Maybe ten minutes passed. I thought about Gobi and her sister and the way it had all come unraveled.

I thought about my dad.

When you're young, you think your father can do anything. Unless he was this severely abusive person and beat you or got drunk and smashed things, you probably worshiped him. At least most of the guys I knew were like that. They might not have used those exact words, but they all have some cherished memory of something they did with their father, even if it was just a shiny, far-off moment.

I remembered being eight years old and making a Pinewood Derby car for Boy Scouts. Dad had brought out a gleaming red Craftsman toolbox that I had never seen before and helped me carve the car out of a block of wood, and we sat at the kitchen table painting it silver and blue with red flames up the side. I drank Pepsi and he sipped a beer. When we finished, the car didn't weigh enough, so we put lead weights in the bottom and sprayed lubricant on the wheels until it rolled freely from one side of the table to the other. I won third place, and he said, "I'm proud of you."

I remembered going fishing with him up in Maine, taking a little motorboat out across the foggy lake until it was too dark to see our bobbers.

I remembered him teaching me how to tie a necktie on the morning of my cousin's wedding.

I remembered seeing him in the stands at my first junior high swimming tournament, standing next to my mom and cheering.

I remembered waking up very early in the morning and hearing him downstairs making coffee before slipping out to work.

I remembered the first time I ever heard him swear.


The light changed again.

The night air was cold and damp. Without a cell phone, I realized that I didn't know what time it was, although I'd probably been standing here for at least ten minutes.

I crossed Eighth Avenue and headed east.

It took me thirty minutes to get across town on foot to the tower on 855 Third Avenue, and another twenty minutes standing up against the glass, waving and gesturing and knocking on the glass until Rufus glanced up from his newspaper and realized who I was. He tucked the paper away and stood up slowly, making his way across the huge marble lobby as if he couldn't quite believe what he was seeing.

"Brother," he said, as he unlocked the door and opened it for me, "you do work odd hours."

I stepped inside and looked around. The only sound was the fountain, clattering out endless watery applause for an audience of two. I caught a glimpse of my reflection in the glass, my bloody tuxedo shirt and bruised face.

"What happened to you?"

"I got mugged," I said. "Did anybody else come through here?"

"What, tonight?" He regarded me doubtfully. "Just the cleaning crew. Couple other security guards, Davy and Rheinhart—they're down in the control room, doing their rounds."

"Nobody else? You're sure?"

"Been at this desk all night." Rufus cocked his head to the side. "You want me to call the cops?"

"No thanks. Is there anybody up on forty-seven?"

"Some of the partners are working late, I guess. Where are you going?"

I went to the turnstile and hopped over it. "Up."

"Hey, man, you ain't supposed to do that. You got to swipe in first. That's policy."

"I lost my wallet, remember?" I headed for the elevators. "Keep your eyes open."

"What am I looking for?" Rufus said distantly. "You sure you don't want me to call you an ambulance or something?"

He was still watching me as the elevator doors slid shut.

I stepped out of the elevator and into the quiet of the climate-controlled hallway. The lights on the forty-seventh floor were turned down to their dimmest setting. In the shadows I saw the letters on the wall spelling out *Harriett, Statham, and Fripp*. Someday, my dad used to say, it would read *Harriett, Statham, Fripp, and Stormaire*. He meant both of us, senior and junior.

I walked through the reception area and gazed out the floor-to-ceiling window at the lights of Midtown far below. The glass was cold, beaded with condensation, my breath ghosting against it and then evaporating again.

The only sound was the faint whir of sleeping electronics, a scanner clicking, a fax machine's far-off hum.

The reception desk had been immaculately tidied up in preparation for Monday morning. Framed personal photos from home, a potted plant, flat-screen monitor cycling through endless screen-savers. Beyond it was the wide opaque glass door leading back into the offices themselves.

I took the handle and tugged.

It was locked.

I shouldn't have been surprised. I took a breath and wondered what I'd come here for anyway. What had I been expecting to find all the way up here, halfway between God and Broadway? The answer to all my questions?

The elevator chimed behind me.

The doors opened. Footsteps padded across the carpet and stopped.

"Perry?"

I looked around at the figure standing on the other side of the reception area, staring back at me.

"Hello, Dad."

# 30

Describe a fictional character. Be sure to point out what you do and do not like about the character and relate these attributes to yourself. (William and Mary)

"What are you doing here?" he asked. "What happened to your face?"

I didn't move. "What are *you* doing here?"

"This is my office."

"It's three a.m."

"You're bleeding," he said. "Were you in some kind of accident?"

"You could say that."

"Well, what happened?"

"Mom said that she was calling you. Did you talk to her?"

"She may have called, I'm not sure." He took out his cell phone, pressed a button, and put it away. "My cell died. I've been on the phone with the police for the last three hours, trying to find you. I came here . . ."—he took a breath and released it—"because I didn't know where else to go."

He took a step toward me, moving closer under the recessed lighting, and this time I took a step back.

"Who's Santamaria?"

"Who?"

"Santamaria."

"I don't know what you're talking about."

"Bullshit."

"Perry, I swear to you, if I had the slightest idea what you were talking about, I would tell you."

"Like you told me about Meredith?"

He was quiet for a moment.

"That was different," he said. "And it's over."

"Whatever."

He tucked his chin and glared at me from underneath his eyebrows, his voice low and intense. "You'd better watch yourself."

"Or what?" I flicked my eyes back to the names on the wall outside. "You're not going to let me be a lawyer? You're not going to let me work here and be like you?" I exhaled. "I think I'd rather clean toilets."

Dad flipped one hand outward, dismissing my words. "I'm sure you would, but that's not an option. Your mother and I have invested too much in your future to let you piss it all away on some act of knee-jerk immaturity." His voice tightened with newfound resolve—he'd regained the parental high ground and wasn't about to lose it again. "Now come with me. I'm taking you home. We can deal with the car and the rest of it in the morning."

"I'm not leaving with you."

"You're mistaken. Badly."

"Don't touch me."

He reached up anyway, gripping my shoulder and arm.

"Get your hands off me." Squirming loose, I tried to take another step back but ran into the door. There was no place left to maneuver.

"Listen to yourself," Dad said. "You're about to burst into tears. Stop this nonsense right now."

*"Get your hands off me, I said!"*

When his hand reached for me again, I punched him in the mouth.

Dad took a step back, blinking at me and touching his lip, staring at the blood that his only son had somehow drawn. He looked more startled than hurt or even angry. It was the expression of a man who'd just been informed that, effective immediately, up was down and black was white.

Neither of us said a word.

"Two things," I said. "First, when I get back to school I'm joining the swim team again. Second, if you ever cheat on Mom again and I find out, I'm going to beat the living shit out of you."

Dad's high forehead creased with the tiniest of frowns. "Are you still on that?"

"You lied to us."

"You don't know the details."

"I know I can't trust you," I said. "What else do I need to know?"

"I don't know, Perry. I don't know who you are anymore."

"Yeah, well, that makes two of us."

Dad's shoulders sagged. He glanced around the reception area as if seeming to remember that he was in an office, a place of negotiation and civility.

"Sit down," he said. "Let's talk."

"Not now." I pointed at the doors leading back into the office. "Do you have a key for this door?"

"I think so. Why?"

"I need you to open it for me."

"What's this all about, Perry?"

"It's about Gobi," I said.

# 31

How has your family history, culture, or environment influenced who you are? (University of Florida)

Dad unlocked the door and we stepped inside. We walked down the freshly vacuumed hallway past a series of closed doors and oak-paneled conference rooms. The darkness seemed to be holding its breath.

"There's no one else here," Dad said.

I didn't say anything. We kept moving forward. At the far end of the hall I turned left at a bank of photocopiers and stopped. Twenty yards away, the lights were on in the corner office. Without looking back at my dad, I padded past the other cubicles until I was standing in front of the door.

My hand went up to try the knob, and a voice spoke up behind me.

"Excuse me? Can I help you with something?"

My shoulders jerked with surprise and I whirled around. Valerie Statham was standing there in a white blouse and skirt, no shoes, and very little makeup. Her hair was down and she looked much older than I remembered from our conversation in the elevator, although it was probably the expression of surprise on her face.

"Phillip?" she said, glancing back at my father. "What are you doing here?" She turned to me. "What is this? What's going on?"

"I . . ." My dad shook his head. "I'm sorry, Valerie, but I honestly don't know."

Valerie took a step back, alternating between my bloody tuxedo and my dad's fat lip. "You two look awful. Is everything all right?"

My dad nodded. "Perry . . ." he started, and I imagined him saying, *Perry and I were just having a private conversation about being responsible.* I imagined him saying, *Perry's just had another one of his famous dizzy spells.* I imagined him saying, *Perry seems to be having some trouble discerning fantasy from reality.*

Instead, he said: "Perry was asking me about someone called Santamaria. Do you have any idea what that means?"

Valerie turned to me. Her eyes narrowed. "Santamaria?"

"Yes."

"No, I can't say that I do."

"Is there anyone else up here?" I asked.

"No."

"How do you know?"

Something changed in Valerie's expression. I couldn't quite tell what it was—I didn't know her that well—but the puzzlement hardened somehow, grew an edge.

She looked at my dad.

"Phillip, may I speak to you privately in my office?"

"Of course," he said.

"No." I grabbed his wrist. "Don't do it. Don't go in there with her."

Now they were both staring at me. Valerie in particular made a point of looking straight into my eyes. "Poor guy, he looks absolutely exhausted. Perry, I enjoyed your show tonight, the little bit of it there was. You were right, your band *is* good. You might want to consider hiring someone else to do the lights, though."

I stared at her.

"It's you," I said.

"I beg your pardon?"

"You're Santamaria."

Valerie didn't react immediately, but when she did, it was with a tight, practiced smile. "Well, I've been called a lot of things over the years, but I believe that's a first. I'm more likely to be the *Nina* or the *Pinta,* don't you think?"

"That's why you came to the bar tonight," I said, "because Gobi was there."

"I'm sorry," Valerie said, "but I honestly—"

"Why did you kill her sister?"

"I assure you, the only thing that I've killed tonight is a bottle of Maalox, and that's only because I drank too much coffee."

"You laundered their money. You did it from here. You're the bank."

"I beg your pardon?"

"Perry," Dad said, "that's *enough.*"

Valerie's smile hadn't changed. "It looks like somebody doesn't want that letter of recommendation to Columbia."

"Dad, just don't go in the office. I don't care how mad you get at me. You can ground me for the rest of my life—let's just go."

"Perry, don't be ridiculous."

Before I could stop them, he went into her office and shut the door. It was quiet for a moment. I heard voices—Valerie's, sounding

calm and logical at first, and my dad's, then Valerie's again, louder—
and I went to the door and tried to open it, but it was locked. Dad
was shouting now. I heard him saying, "What are you talking about?
*What does that mean?*"

There was a sudden thump, a crash of furniture overturning.
What sounded like piles of books thumped to the floor. The door
handle started rattling hard from the other side, but it didn't open.

"Dad!" I shouted. "Open up!"

A second later I heard the shot.

# 32

Sometimes being proven right isn't the most satis-
fying outcome to a situation. Discuss one situation where you were right and wish that you hadn't
been. (University of Chicago)

Flashpoint:

My dad stumble-tripping backwards out of the office, fingers
laced across his stomach, falling down between the copy machine
and the cubicle beside it. His blood splashed on the oatmeal-colored
carpet like an abstract painting.

Flashpoint:

Valerie, stepping calmly forward, getting ready to shoot him
again.

Flashpoint:

Me, lunging at her, pulling her arms down as her elbow angled
up and jabbed me in the eye.

Recovering my balance, grabbing my father, legs pumping hard
back through the office in the direction we'd come.

Another gunshot from behind.

The glass door in front of us exploding in a spray of glass, revealing the reception area beyond it.

Flashpoint: the elevator fifty feet in front of us, opening.

And then—

Gobi.


I stayed down, flattened against the carpet, head swiveled toward my father. Bullets exploded above me, smashing into walls and glass and furniture, tearing apart lamps and blowing a computer off the desk. Somewhere to my left I saw Valerie Statham spin around and fire repeatedly at Gobi or at least in the direction where Gobi had come from, the elevators, the entryway. Big wads of stuffing from the gutted chairs and sofa cushions spilled down into the carpet. Splinters of wood flew past my face and got stuck in my hair.

My hearing died again, but I still felt the vibrations of gunfire. The air smelled poisonous. My eyes stung with smoke. My tongue tasted like dirty iodine. I crawled under a desk and slithered to the corner where my dad had drawn his knees up to his chin, his head down.

"Dad?" I shouted, and even though it was loud enough to hurt my throat, I couldn't hear a sound. "Dad? *Dad?*"

He lifted his head, but his face was far away, addled with confusion and fear. I looked at the gunshot wound in his stomach and saw that it had just grazed his side. What remained was superficial but still bleeding steadily.

*"We have to get out of here!"* I silent-shouted. *"Dad, we need to—"*

Something flashed in front of me and crashed to the floor—some object, a fire extinguisher or a monitor, thrown hard, aimed at my face. Warm fingers seized my wrist. Hot steel rammed into my ear. I saw Valerie Statham's bloody face staring up at me, her lips shaping the words *Get up*.

Before I could get to my feet, she dragged me forward through the broken glass and smoke, clamped her fingers around my throat, and held me up in front of her as a shield.

Non-noises pressed against my ears, the vibration of sound I couldn't hear. Very faintly I heard voices shouting and saw Gobi twenty feet in front of me, still holding the sawed-off shotgun and the machine pistol that she'd taken from the men back on Tenth Avenue.

She was completely soaked in blood. Her hair swung in red tangles around her shoulders, and her face was a gleaming mask, her eyes like hard diamonds.

*I am Death.*

"The police are already on their way up," Valerie's voice shouted behind me. "You'll never get out of here. They'll be looking for a psychotic Lithuanian girl who just gunned down an attorney and his son. I should just kill you now."

Gobi grinned and I saw the gap where her tooth had been knocked out. She said something in Lithuanian.

Then she shot me.

# 33

Describe a painful experience and what you learned from it. (Boston College)

Gobi's bullet tore through my leg just below the knee, cutting a trough along the outer margin of the calf muscle. The instant it hit, Valerie let go of me, shoving me forward. I plunged straight down, facefirst, into a bath of pain so intense that I couldn't even scream.

Not that it would've mattered. Nobody heard a thing. My abused eardrums registered only the faintest thumps and pops, like fireworks from the next county over. The elevators behind Gobi were opening again, and I saw cops or security guards piling out. Their faces looked exactly like what you would expect on anyone walking into the middle of a firefight. It took about three seconds for them to duck and cover behind the nearest couch.

"Drop it!" one of the cops shouted. "Drop the gun!"

Gobi didn't move. She stood twenty feet in front of me, keeping the machine pistol raised in my direction so they could see it, the sawed-off shotgun hanging at her side. Lifting one arm, she wiped the blood from her face.

"You shot me," I said.

*"Put the gun down now!"*

Ignoring the cops, Gobi walked over to where I was lying and bent down by my ear.

"Perry," she said, "I had a very nice time tonight."

"You're unbelievable."

"I had to shoot you."

"Why?"

"I had to get you out of the way."

I hoisted myself up on one arm and craned my neck to see Valerie Statham sprawled against the reception desk, chin tucked, one arm folded awkwardly behind her. Her eyes were still open. She looked like a broken swan. A curl of smoke drifted from the hole just above her left breast.

*"Put the gun down now!"*

Still focused on me, Gobi pushed the barrel of the machine pistol into my chest. "You need to stand up."

"I can't."

"You need to. I cannot carry your weight."

"You should have thought of that . . . before you shot me in the *leg.*"

"Come on, Perry. Be a man."

She pulled me upward. Somehow I managed to get up on my good leg, leaning against the barrel of the machine pistol. The agony didn't hurt too much. The two of us staggered around until I saw the two cops behind the couch, both pointing a gun at us.

"Let him go."

She shook her head. "He is coming with me."

"Lady, there's no way you're getting out of here. There's about fifty cops down in the lobby. Just let him go."

Gobi pivoted and opened fire. The machine pistol rattled hard against the plate-glass window that formed the west wall of the firm's reception area, and it shattered into big toothy jags and slices, exploding open to expose the night, six hundred feet in the air. Cold wind flooded in, blowing debris and papers everywhere, swirling them out into the darkness. Suddenly we weren't indoors anymore; we were outside with Manhattan underneath us.

Gobi gave me a gap-toothed grin. "Trust me?"

"Are you kidding?"

"How far can you jump?"

I stared at her. "What—?"

She dragged me across the reception area, foot by foot, closer to the blown-apart window, never budging the gun from its place against my abdomen. Air buffeted my tuxedo and flustered my hair. My leg felt like it was on fire. Somewhere behind us the cops were both yelling the same stuff over and over again, things they were trained to say when they saw the situation going from bad to worse.

I could see over the edge now, looking down. "I'm not doing this!" I shouted.

"We have no other choice."

"You're kidding, right?"

"No, Perry."

"I'm not jumping."

"Then you will die."

I nodded to the gaping hole on the forty-seventh floor. "How is this not dying?"

Gobi gave me another nudge toward the edge and for a second I actually felt the vacuum of space itself sucking me outward. For the first time I registered the arrival of something out there, huge and loud, eclipsing the city lights. It was bigger than my father, bigger than college. It was as if the final seconds of my life had been waiting for me here this whole time and now that it had arrived I had no choice about how to meet it.

Outside the building, a high-pitched turbine whine thundered up into view, and that was when I saw the helicopter.

"Get ready!" Gobi shouted.

The helicopter tilted toward us, lowering.

Gobi grabbed me and jumped.

# 34

If you had one day left to live, how would you spend it and why? (University of Southern California)

We landed in the helicopter with a thud.

I didn't hear it, but I realized right away that I wasn't falling anymore. I was rolling on my side across a series of carpeted bumps, my leg shrieking at me with every point of contact. I would have screamed, but I wasn't breathing. Not yet.

When I finally managed to inhale, the air smelled like cold leather upholstery and diesel exhaust. Curved walls and four beige seats rose up on either side of me, illuminated by soft recessed lighting. There were seatbelts and cup holders. Looking back one last time, I caught a bleary glimpse of the skyscraper's broken window already swinging away from us, turning as the helicopter's hatch drew shut, and then everything became muffled and lower, a pulsing *whop-whop-whop* that resonated through my chest cavity.

I drew my leg up, pressing both hands against the damp fabric of my pants, and crawled up into one of the bucket seats next to Gobi, who was hunched forward with her head turned away, looking out the opposite window. I poked experimentally at my knee. At least the bleeding had stopped. What was left was a shallow gouge outside my kneecap, and although it still hurt worse than anything I'd ever gone through, including five years ago when my appendix had burst in the middle of the night, I realized that I could probably stand it. I straightened the leg, bracing myself for a dose of world-ending pain. The end of the world didn't come.

I leaned over and saw the shadowy form of the pilot illuminated by the lights of the cockpit and redirected my attention to Gobi.

"Who's flying this thing?"

The lump next to me didn't move.

"Gobi."

When she still didn't sit up or answer, I reached over and took hold of her arm, giving it a not-so-gentle squeeze. She let out a soft groan and peered at me, two frazzled green eyes behind a wild thatch of blood-stiffened hair. The breath in her lungs sounded like what you'd hear by blowing through a clogged garden hose. Her gaze looked foggy and dull.

Then abruptly she smiled, as if recognizing that I was next to her.

"Perry."

"How are you doing?"

"Not bad." She nodded. "I am just very tired."

"Yeah," I said, "you call that kind of tired getting shot in the chest."

"Nothing serious."

"Bullshit." I listened to the space between words. The wheezing noise was getting worse. "Gobi—"

"I will be fine, Perry. I gave myself another EpiPen injection in the elevator. I have survived worse."

"Gobi, listen. You can't just keep giving yourself adrenaline shots. You need serious medical attention."

"And I will get it. As soon as we arrive at our destination."

"Where are we going?" I looked out at the city of Manhattan spread out below us. "I'm pretty sure this thing won't go all the way back to Lithuania."

"The pilot is a friend. I arranged it beforehand as an insurance policy. He'll get us out of here."

"Where to?"

She scowled. "Do you always ask so many questions?"

"My guidance counselor says it's the sign of an intellectually curious mind."

"Perry?"

"What?"

"Do you . . ."—another wheezing gurgle—"hate me?"

"Hate you?" I blinked at her. "Just because you dragged me all over New York City on prom night and made me an accomplice to murder five times over, then shot me?" I said. "Why would I hate you?"

"We could try to start over."

"I think it's a little late for that."

"I am sorry about your father."

"He'll be okay. The bullet just grazed him." I glanced down at my knee again and tried not to think about how hard she was laboring to breathe. "I guess we both could've been a lot worse off."

Gobi didn't say anything for a long time. Manhattan's lights shimmied off into the distance as we crossed over Long Island Sound, skimming north. Warm air had begun to circulate through the ventilation system, and I felt my muscles beginning to sink into the upholstered seats. Fatigue from the adrenaline comedown began seeping through every fiber of my body, overtaking me by inches and then by feet.

"Seriously, Perry," Gobi's voice said, from what sounded very far away. "Whatever happens, I hope you get everything that you want out of life. You deserve it."

"Well," I said, turning away, "thanks."

"I mean it, Perry. What happened tonight was not easy, but it had to be done. I could not have done it without you." She reached up and brushed one hand over my face, her palm cold and damp. "My sister would have thanked you too."

"The first Gobija."

"Yes."

I rolled my forehead against the cold glass windows, hoping for a degree of sanity. I told myself that what I was thinking was crazy. I tried saying the words to myself, just so I could hear how ridiculous it was, but it didn't work. I wouldn't be satisfied until I spoke them out loud.

"Gobi."

A whistling inhalation. "What?"

"I can't believe I'm about to say this, but . . . you know, I could still be your hostage."

She cocked one eyebrow, the expression of comic incredulity at stark odds with her pale, perspiring face. "What are you talking about?"

"For a little while longer, you could use me to get out of here. You know, hold on to me." I nodded at the sawed-off shotgun she'd brought with her; the machine pistol must have stayed back at the office, before the jump. "You've still got a gun. The cops won't stop you if they think you're going to kill me. Then once you get, you know . . . on an airplane or wherever, you could let me go."

"That's a very generous offer," she said. "But I'll be fine."

"No, you won't."

"Trust me."

"Quit saying that."

She smiled and sat back for the rest of the ride. Despite everything, I felt my eyelids getting heavy, helpless against exhaustion. Time drifted, blurring, an abstraction of darkness and white noise.

I jerked awake.

The helicopter was descending.

"Where are we?"

Gobi sat forward, her voice hardly a croak. "See for yourself."

Looking down, I saw my house.

Use this space to tell us anything about yourself that you think we might have overlooked. Be creative. Have fun! (Columbia University)

From above, my house was a blazing electric sea of blue and red emergency lights. I saw state police cruisers snaked halfway up the street. It was four thirty in the morning and the neighbors were outside in their bathrobes and jackets, standing in the yard. There were news vans on the lawn.

"What are we doing here?" I asked.

Gobi ignored me and shouted something to the pilot in Lithuanian. The helicopter went into a low hover, shaking the poplars and shrubbery, blasting newly formed leaves from the trees and whipping them through the neighborhood. A spotlight speared down from the helicopter's undercarriage and hit the roof. I saw shingles flipping and flying loose.

Now I could recognize faces: Mr. Drobenack, who always complained about the property line, Mr. and Mrs. Englebrook, who always let their dogs poop on our yard, all using their hands to shield their eyes from the light.

"Hang on."

Gobi threw open the hatchway. Noise roared in on a fresh gush of cold night air, pushing me back into my seat. Bracing herself against the bulkhead, Gobi reached up into a cargo swing bin and brought down a canvas bundle, opening the flaps and tossing it out. I leaned sideways and saw a rope ladder unfurling downward until it was dangling just above my roof.

"Hold it a second!" I shouted. "What are you doing?"

"I have to get the bomb out of your basement."

"What?"

*"I said I have to get the bomb out of your basement!"*

"Wait," I said, "maybe—"

She gripped the ladder and swung out, already gone.

I stood in the hatchway watching her repel down, a small dark shape swaying and weaving in the prop-wash until she dropped down onto the top of our house. A moment passed while she checked her balance, gauged the slope of the roof, then scurried across it toward the nearest bedroom window, flung it open, and crawled inside. It was her room, the one we'd given her to stay in. Of course she would have left it unlocked.

The helicopter had already started to lift. I reached forward and tapped the pilot on the shoulder.

"Where are we going?"

He either didn't understand or chose to ignore the question, and it didn't really matter because a minute later we were descending again, this time over a ball field at the other end of my subdivision. Even as we came to ground, the pilot didn't say anything. But when we touched down, he pointed at the door and made an odd, flicking-away motion with his hands that I realized I knew from earlier.

"Morozov?" I shouted, over the engine's roar. "Pasha?"

He jerked around and looked at me, the ratlike, emaciated face and hungry eyes gazing from deep inside their sockets.

"You knew everything the whole time?"

"What do you think?"

"You were going to chop my fingers off!"

Morozov paused to give the matter some thought. "No," he said finally, "not really."

"If you knew I was lying to you the whole time, why didn't you say anything?"

"Gobija wanted to test you. She likes her men to prove themselves, to know if she can trust them." He shrugged. "You passed the test."

"What if I'd failed?"

"Never mind." He gestured at the door. "Get out."

"You did all this for her?"

"You are not the only one who loves her."

"Whoa," I said. "Who said anything about loving her?"

He glared at me as if I'd insulted his entire family ancestry. A closer look revealed that his eyes were red, his cheeks streaked and shining with long silvery-looking creases that followed the natural etchings of his face. After a second I realized that he was crying.

"Get out," he repeated, and this time I did. I had already jumped down and made my way across the baseball diamond, back toward my street, the helicopter roaring back overhead, when I realized that his accent wasn't Russian at all. I should have recognized it right away; I'd heard enough of it that night.

It was Lithuanian.

# 36

What individual, alive or dead, had the single greatest influence on your life, and why? (George Washington University)

From what people said, the news footage they ran for weeks afterward showed everything very clearly, although I never watched it. I didn't have to. I was there.

I couldn't really afford to run back through my neighborhood, but I did anyway, forcing my leg to move faster past the houses that I'd known all my life, homes that I'd biked past and delivered newspapers to, familiar mailboxes and sidewalks, trees and landmarks, until I got to my street. It all looked different now, even my own house, as if I were seeing it from a totally different set of eyes. It seemed like I'd been away a lot longer than ten hours.

"Perry?"

My mom broke out of a crowd of people and ran toward me, throwing her arms around me and hugging me. "Oh, thank God. Are you all right? What happened to your leg?"

"It's a long story," I said. "Is Annie okay?"

"Annie's fine. She's at the Espenshades'. I think she's finally asleep."

I turned to look at our house. "Where's Gobi? Has she come out yet?"

A peculiar gleam flashed through Mom's face, as if she had just now understood something she felt she should have noticed a long time ago. "No," she said. "Perry, how did you get back from the city?"

"On the helicopter."

"She brought you with her? Who *is* she, Perry?"

"She's just a girl."

"Annie said you told her—"

"Forget what I told Annie. I was wrong. I didn't know anything about her at all."

Mom stood next to me, not talking, not moving. After a long time she drew in one of those breaths that I could tell meant that she wanted to say something but wasn't sure how to phrase it.

"I got a message from your father. He's at Beth Israel. They were going to take him to surgery but apparently he's refusing until they transfer him to New York Presbyterian. Stubborn to the last, that man."

"Uh-huh."

"And now . . ." Exasperation trickled into her voice, making the whole conversation more familiar. "The police won't even let us in our own *house*. The bomb squad came and they couldn't find anything, so they left, but now I want to know—"

"Wait a second," I said. "The bomb squad didn't find anything in the basement?"

"Not in the basement, not in the whole house," Mom said. "They brought dogs and everything. Then they just picked up and left again, but they still won't let us go back inside—"

"So there was no bomb?"

"Apparently not."

I turned and looked back at the house, amazed.

*Trust me.*

"Damn," I said.

"What is it?"

"Nothing, it's just that she was bluffing after a—"

At that second there was a blast and bright flame shuddered up from the house where I'd grown up, blowing the windows out in a tinkling spray. A second later the roof blew off and the walls exploded, showering debris outward as the house caved in, collapsing in a heap.

# 37

If you had the opportunity to start your life over, what would you change? What would you keep the same? (George Washington University)

*Blown Away.*

"That's the headline?" Mom asked, picking up the *New York Post* sitting next to Dad's hospital bed. "That's what it says?"

I watched as my dad reached out over the bedrail, past the newspaper, and picked up a cup of coffee. He sniffed it, recoiled, and put it back without taking a drink. Apparently he'd been complaining to his nurses about the coffee since he'd arrived here. My impression was that they couldn't wait to get rid of him and send him back to Starbucks so they wouldn't have to listen to him whine anymore.

"Well," Dad said with kind of a shrug, "it's true."

"At least Perry wasn't blown away!" Mom said.

"Perry wasn't in the house, Mom," Annie said. She didn't look up from her phone, her thumbs clicking busily away. "Check this out: this TV station in Japan wants to interview Perry."

"No interviews," Dad said. "Not until they finish the investigation."

"Dad, come on! It's in Tokyo! They're interested in us!"

"You heard your father," Mom said. "No interviews."

"Mom, that's so mean! Nobody's ever going to care this much about me again!"

"That's not true, honey," Mom said, not looking up from the newspaper. "We'll always care about you."

She rolled her eyes. "Gee, thanks."

I sat in the corner of the room without talking, letting myself disappear behind a cloud of flowers and balloons, get-well cards, and loud, overlapping voices. The only thing that didn't seem to belong here was the hospital room itself. It would have been more appropriately suited to someone who was actually fighting for his life, or at least trying to get well. My eyes kept going back to the *Post* headline running in huge capital letters above the aerial photo of our house, or what had been our house, blasted to pieces and burned to the ground.

*Blown away.*

I dreamed about you sometimes.

In my dreams we were walking down Tenth Avenue together in the dark. You hadn't been shot after all, and we were both all right. I asked you if you were done, and you said yes, it was finished.

In my dreams the streetlights all went off as we walked past them, but I could still see perfectly clearly to the corner. There was heat and light pouring out of you like a lantern, shining down the sidewalk in front of us, filling the intersection with amazing white light. When I reached for your hand you let me keep it there and smiled.

You kissed me one more time. In my dreams I always knew that meant that I was about to wake up. The light spilling out of your face and eyes and skin blazed up higher, and you said you had to go.

You said it had to be this way.

You said you were a goddess of fire.


Life went on.

It always did, and that summer was no exception. Within six weeks of having the property cleared and sold, Mom and Dad had met with architects and agreed on a piece of land for the new house. Everybody was relieved. It would be in the same school district for Annie, and the insurance settlement had been very generous. Mom said she'd wanted a new kitchen anyway.

Gradually the reporters started leaving us alone, and that was a big relief too. We spent the beginning of that summer holed up in a five-star Connecticut resort with a pool, sauna, and day spa, eating in restaurants and picking out all new clothing, furniture, pots and pans . . . everything you need to buy when someone blows up your house.

Dad insisted on getting the best of everything. He said that Mom deserved it (but never said exactly why). After what happened with Valerie "Santamaria" Statham, I had expected his stress level to go through the roof, but true to his habit of surprising everybody, he tendered his resignation and just walked away "to pursue other opportunities." He said it was like a weight had been lifted from his shoulders. The preliminary investigation had revealed that nobody else at the firm, including my dad, had any idea what Valerie had been involved in, but by then Harriet, Statham, and Fripp had become the Enron of the legal world, a late-night talk show joke, and their client list had emptied out faster than the first-class cabins on the *Titanic*. Throughout it all, Dad remained weirdly philosophical about the whole thing. "Never feel sorry for an attorney with a book deal," he said, and when Mom asked him if he really had a book deal, he just winked and said that he was "in talks with publishers."

It was a little odd having him around more often, but a good kind of strange, like having a three-month vacation in your own home-town. We played tennis, talked more, argued less, and spent ten days on the beach up in Maine. My mother laughed more. She and Dad started holding hands. Annie got asked out on her first date—nothing formal, just a group of friends going out to a movie together, al-though the boy who asked her came up to the door himself to pick her up while his mother waited out in the car. I still remember his face when he looked through the hotel suite door, his eyes wide with amazement when he said, "Geez, you guys actually *live* here?"

I got together with Norrie and the other guys in Inchworm and we jammed a couple times, but Interscope Records never called, and by July, Sasha had quit to go start his own band.

I watched the scar starting to form on my knee. No matter how tan I got, it stayed white.

Gradually, the dreams stopped.

By late July, when I still hadn't heard from Columbia, I assumed that I'd gone from the waitlist to the trash can. Didn't bother me as much as I'd expected. I was in at Uconn and Trinity. I'd started to wonder if that was what I really wanted after all.

And then, a few days later, the phone rang.

# 38

If finances and family considerations were not an
issue, how would you spend your last summer before
starting college? (Rutgers)

The woman in the hallway introduced herself as Leanne Couzens,
head of Undergraduate Admissions at Columbia University. She
was a brunette in her midforties, with an ice-cool confidence that
probably came with holding the fate of thousands of panicked high
school graduates in her clutches. I knew right away that Dad liked
her by the way he reached right in past Mom to shake her hand,
before she even got a chance to invite us into her office.

"Please," she said, "have a seat. Can I get anybody anything,
water or a cup of coffee?"

"I think we're fine, thanks," Dad said.

Leanne sat down on the opposite side of a polished granite-topped
desk, the elegant surface of which was disturbed by nothing more
than a laptop computer, a telephone, and a silver-framed photo with
its back to us. The rest of the office was just as streamlined, with a
single chrome bookshelf and a view of the street outside—it would

have been completely sterile if it hadn't been for the plants hanging in the window, dangling down like long green spiders.

"Well," she said. "As I mentioned earlier when we spoke on the phone, this is highly unorthodox. Normally the admissions process is conducted completely online. I haven't actually interviewed a prospective student in . . . well, a very long time." She smiled at me, and I felt myself smiling back, almost involuntarily. "But Perry is a special case. It was actually my idea to invite you here."

"Well," Mom said, "we certainly appreciate Columbia's interest in Perry."

Leanne chuckled. "I hardly think I'm the only one interested in Perry. According to what's been reported on the news the past two months . . . well, you've certainly found yourself in the limelight, haven't you?"

"Yes, ma'am," I said, not sure how I should feel about the way she pronounced the word *limelight*. "I mean, I guess so."

"I should say that you have. A tragic ending for Ms. Zaksauskas, certainly, but . . . well, in any case, I know you're busy, so let's get right to it, shall we?" She opened a desk drawer and brought out a folder, opening it. "Let's see. We received your application back in May. GPA was three point three . . ."

"Three point three four," Dad chimed in.

"Three point three four." Leanne's smile tightened a bit at the edges as she picked up a sharpened pencil and made a small mark on the page. "Right, of course. SAT scores were twenty-two hundred, twenty-five on the ACT, squarely in the eighty-fifth percentile. Member of the swim team, debate, and forensics, participant in Student Senate—all very respectable . . ."—another smile, slightly altered—"but, as I'm sure you know, Columbia's undergraduate program is known for being exceptionally selective. Because of our standards of excellence, we can afford to be picky. And Mr. and Mrs. Stormaire, please don't take this the wrong way, but if these numbers represented the totality of Perry's application, well . . . we wouldn't be sitting here together."

I glanced back at Mom and Dad. Neither one of them was smiling anymore, although Dad was giving it his best, somewhat constipated effort.

"I'm sorry," Mom said, "I'm not sure I know what you're talking about."

"I'm talking about this." Leanne's hand went back to the drawer and reappeared with a two-inch-thick stack of paper, dropping it on the desk with a thump. "Perry's essay."

My parents frowned, both of them looking at the pile of pages as if it were some bloated fungus that Leanne had plucked out of the ground and dropped in front of their noses. For a second it was amazing how much they looked alike.

"That's his essay?" Mom asked.

"Mmm." Leanne flipped through the pages. "Our application asks for a statement of two hundred and fifty to five hundred words on a given topic. Perry's was forty thousand words long."

"Forty *thousand?*" Dad asked.

"What was the topic?" Mom asked.

Leanne glanced down at the first folder she'd opened. "Discuss a situation or event that helped shape your understanding of your own identity." She blinked up at us, feigning incredulity so perfectly that I wondered if she practiced in the mirrored surface of her desktop. "Now, under normal circumstances, an essay that so completely disregarded our standard submission criteria would be returned unread and the applicant would either be invited to resubmit a more appropriate personal statement or simply told that he or she is probably not a good fit for the undergraduate program. In this case, however, the sheer length of the essay caught the attention of one of our admissions officers, who passed it along to the others . . . It's achieved a kind of cult status around here, actually."

"Cult status?" Mom asked, staring at me now. "What did he write about?"

"I suppose the simplest way to describe it is as a kind of narrative of his night in New York with Gobija Zaksauskas," Leanne said, letting the pages flip through her fingers. "What Perry sent in along with his application was a long, rambling narrative full of inappropriate language and criminal behavior with very little, if any, regard to the criteria normally applied to a standard college admission essay. It was colloquial, meandering, contradictory, and sometimes downright sloppy." She let the top page flip shut. "It's also one of the most compelling and original pieces of writing that I've ever seen in this department."

"Well," Dad said.

"*Well,*" Mom said.

"Yes," Leanne said, staring straight at me. "Well. Perry. By now I hope it's clear why I took the initiative to invite you and your family here personally?"

"Yes, ma'am," I said. "I guess it is."

"Good." Holding the edges of the essay with her fingertips, she slid it exactly six inches to the left. "Then I suppose the only thing left to say is, Welcome to Columbia."

Silence surrounded me, very clear and still. I could feel my parents' eyes on me, waiting.

"Thank you," I said. "But I don't think that's what I want right now."

Leanne didn't move, except to tilt her head very slightly to the left. "Excuse me?"

"I've been thinking." I took in a breath and let it out. "I think that what I really want to do is take a year off before I start college—"

"A year off?" Dad said. "Wait a minute. This wasn't what we discussed."

"I was thinking I would travel. You know, go abroad for a while. See the world."

"I see," Leanne said. She was still blinking, and a faint reddish color had begun to rise into her cheeks and the back of her neck. "Well. That's certainly one alternative."

"Honey?" Mom said. "Are you sure this is what you want?"

"Positive," I said.

"No, he isn't," Dad said, and turned back to Leanne, already halfway out of his chair. "Ms. Couzens, I apologize for this. Can you excuse us for a moment?"

"No, Dad."

He stared at me. "Perry—"

"Dad. *No.*" I stood up and held out my hand. "I'm glad you liked my essay, Leanne. Thanks for your time."

"No problem at all," she said. "I meant what I said about your writing, Perry. And I hope that if you change your mind, you'll keep us . . . well, in mind."

"I will," I said, and turned to my parents. "Ready?"

My mom stood on the front steps while my dad went to get the car. The August sun beat down on our faces, feeling considerably hotter after the air-conditioned office, the car-exhaust humidity held in by the tall buildings on either side of the street.

"He's mad," I said.

She frowned. "He'll get over it."

"When, do you think?"

"Well . . ." She pulled her sunglasses out and put them on. "Let's just say maybe it's a good idea that you're going away for a while."

I laughed. After a moment, she did too. "I'm proud of you, Perry."

"You are?"

"And although your father might not say so, he is too. It takes something special to realize that the preconceived choices and beliefs that you've always had aren't necessarily the best ones for you. It's not easy."

I turned around and looked back at the building that we'd just left. A few students were scattered around the steps, dressed in shorts and T-shirts, flip-flops and barefoot. Up at the top step, a girl with short blond hair and huge black sunglasses was looking back down at me.

Not just looking, I realized. She was staring.

I felt my heart stop.

"Perry?" Mom said. "What are you doing?"

"I'll be right back."

I could see the steps, but I couldn't feel myself climbing them. When I got to the top, the girl was still peering at me. Now she had to tilt her head upward, and I saw the faint white scar across her neck. The half-heart pendant glinted in the light.

"Excuse me," I said. "Do I know you?"

She paused and shook her head. "Do you go to this school?"

"No."

"Neither do I."

"Then I must have been mistaken."

"Relax." She raised one shoulder. "It happens."

"I'm actually planning to do some traveling. Hike around and see some things before I do any more school."

"Traveling?"

"Yeah. I was thinking Europe, maybe."

She nodded. "Europe is nice."

"I've never been."

"Venice in particular."

"Really?"

"There is a bar called Harry's."

"I've heard of that," I said.

"The bartenders are good at delivering messages," she said. "Perhaps you ought to check with them, if you get over there."

"I will."

"Perry!" my mom's voice shouted up from the curb. "Your father's here!"

"Okay." I turned to wave where the Jaguar was swinging up to the curb. "I'll be right down."

When I looked back, she was gone.

## ACKNOWLEDGMENTS

Writing a novel isn't quite as unnerving as answering college essay questions, but I had a lot of help along the way. Thanks to Rob Swartwood, who read the first draft and went through it with me page by page over a massive plate of rhino fries. Thank you to Phyllis Westberg and Don Laventhall, and to my brilliant and utterly charming editor, Margaret Raymo. On the West Coast, I want to thank Lis Rowinski, Josh Schwartz, and Stephanie Savage, along with Irene Yeung and Roy Lee, for their continued enthusiasm and vision. Ultimately, finally and always, I owe everything good in my life to my wife, Christina, who read the manuscript in one sitting and refused to ever let me give up on the cockeyed ideas that sent me down to the basement every day with nothing but a cup of coffee and a prayer. *As myliu, tave mano brangioji.*

Turn the page for a sneak peek at
Perry and Gobi's next wild adventure in

## *PERRY'S KILLER PLAYLIST*!

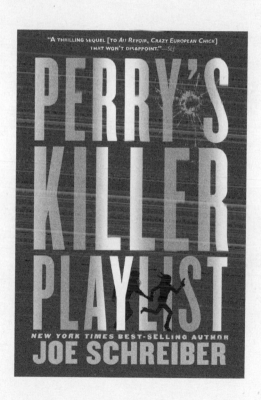

# Prologue:
# "American Idiot" — Green Day

"Don't kill me."

*Nine hundred feet up in the November wind, it's hard to enunciate properly, especially with the barrel of a Glock nine-millimeter jammed in your mouth. They don't tell you these things on the Travel Channel.*

*Gobi takes the automatic out from between my lips. Her eyes sparkle and shine. I think about what she told me back in Venice, what she said at the hotel that night. That all seems like a long time ago now.*

*She smiles, blood and lipstick smeared over her face. Down below, blue lights on the Champ de Mars flash off the steel framework of the Eiffel Tower, warping in the rain. Over her shoulder I can see the gendarmes on the other side of the observation platform with automatic weapons, yelling at us in the language of love. I remember just enough from two years in Mrs. Garvey's French class to decipher "police" and "surrender."*

"As tave myliu," *Gobi says. With her free hand, she reaches out and brushes the wet hair out of my eyes. Her fingers are ice cold.* "Your *hair is getting shaggy,* mielasis.*" Then she points the pistol back at my head.*

"*Just tell me what you've done with my family.*" I'm begging now, and I don't care how it sounds. "*Just tell me where they are.*"

"*I am so sorry, Perry.*" An almost inaudible click as she switches off the safety. "Au revoir."

# 1

# "All These Things That I've Done"

## —The Killers

"Miss me?" she asked.

I leaned forward to kiss the ice cream from her upper lip—maple fudge ripple, arguably the best flavor in the known universe. We were standing barefoot next to the picnic tables by the Twin Star on Route 26, watching the gray waves of October rolling up and crashing on the shore.

Me and Paula.

It was fall, the best time of the year for this battered stretch of shoreline that Connecticut shares with the sea. All around us, the rest of the beach was deserted, a long, unhurried curve of sand, eel grass and wooden fence slats bullied and pushed over sideways by decades of rough Atlantic weather. During the summer this place was mobbed with families and kids, teenagers, bikers, couples—my parents had even come up here on a date once, according to family lore. Now it all felt pleasantly haunted, the parking lot almost empty, the restrooms already locked up for the season, leaving the two of us and the guy behind the ice cream counter just itching to put up his handwritten SEE YOU NEXT SUMMER! sign in the window.

High above us, seagulls squeaked and wheeled in the gunmetal sky, sounding lost and far away.

Paula hugged herself and shivered. "It's chilly."

"Here." I took off my Columbia sweatshirt and wrapped it around her shoulders. "Better?"

"Always the gentleman." She smiled and looked down at the beach, her cell phone still clutched in her hand from the call that she'd just finished. "So, do you want to hear the big news?"

"I thought you'd never tell me."

"I thought you'd never ask."

"Officially asking."

"I just got off the phone with Armitage . . . and he wants to book Inchworm . . ."—she paused, making me wait an extra split-second—". . . for the whole tour."

"Europe?"

"Twelve cities in eighteen days."

"No way." I laughed, and she grabbed me, and I hugged her, lifting her up off her feet and spinning her around. "Paula, that's unbelievable."

"I know!" Her smile had blossomed into a full-out grin, and I looked at all eleven of the sun freckles across the bridge of her nose. I'd counted them when we were waiting in line for one of the rides at Six Flags last month.

"How did that happen?"

"I told you the new songs were great, Perry. Armitage heard your demo and flipped." Now she was clutching my hands, bouncing up and down on her tiptoes with excitement. Her toenails were painted a very dark shade of plum, almost black, and they looked great against the sand, ten little black keys, like the kind you use to play ragtime. "He's booking you guys on a twelve-city tour, starting in London on the twenty-ninth, then Venice, Paris, Madrid . . ." Paula got out her phone, clicking up the screen. "I've got all the dates here."

"This is amazing," I said. "I can't wait to see Europe with you."

She sighed softly, and her shoulders sagged a little. "I wish."

"Wait—you're not coming?"

"Armitage needs me here in New York. And I've got to be back in the studio at the beginning of December. Moby's recording a new album in L.A., and . . ." She saw my expression. "Hey, maybe I can sneak out to Paris for a weekend."

"I'd like that."

"Perry, this is a huge step for you guys. If this works out . . ."

I smiled. "I couldn't have done it without you."

"Oh, shut up."

"I'm serious," I said. "You made this happen."

"Well, that's sweet of you to say." Her blue eyes sparkled, appearing and disappearing as her hair blew in front of her face. She'd spent most of the summer in L.A. and somehow held on to her tan into the fall, so that her blond hair looked even blonder by comparison. "But we all know who really deserves the credit."

"Stop it."

"You wrote all of those new songs, Perry."

"Norrie and I wrote them together."

"Then you and Norrie are the next Lennon and McCartney," she said. "And now the entire European Union is going to find that out for themselves."

"This is amazing."

"I know." She frowned a little, seeing the hint of apprehension in my eyes. "What?"

"Nothing—it's just great news."

"Stormaire . . ."

I smiled. "I just wish you could go with me, that's all."

"You're adorable." She kissed me again, and the kiss lingered this time, her mouth warm and soft against mine, her hair tickling my ears.

"I know."

She stood there looking at me. We'd been dating for less than three months, but I'd told her everything, and she could read me like a book.

"Europe's a big continent, Perry."

"I know."

"You don't even know if she's there."

"Right."

"It's not like you're going to run into her."

"I never said—"

"You didn't have to."

"I wasn't even thinking it."

"There's a reason why I'm not sending you guys to Lithuania," Paula said, and squeezed my hand. "Come on. I'm cold. Let's walk."

# 2

# "Ever Fallen in Love"

## —Buzzcocks

Paula and I had met back in the beginning of August, at a party in Park Slope, not long after I'd seen Gobi for the last time on the steps at Columbia. It turned out that I didn't really know a lot of people at the party, one of those friend-of-a-friend-who-wasn't-really-a-friend type of things. Someone kept playing old Elton John tracks on the iPod docking station, and I was in the process of saying my goodbyes when a voice I'd never heard before said, "Hey."

That was how she'd started out, as a voice over my shoulder, sounding raspy and unfamiliar and amused. "You're that guy," the voice said.

I turned around to look at her, my brain immediately struggling to crunch the numbers. Laid out on the chalkboard, it would've gone something like this:

```
(blond hair) + (blue eyes) x (killer body)
= don't even try
```

Yet here was this woman, a little older than I was and a whole lot hotter, not only looking at me but actually seeming interested.

"I'm sorry?"

"I saw your picture in the *Post*," she said. "You're Perry Stormaire, right?"

"Yeah."

"You're the guy whose house got blown up."

"Uh-huh."

"That was insane."

"Yes," I said, because I never know what to say in these situations. She was referring to what happened on the night of my senior prom, three months before, when the Lithuanian foreign exchange that had been living in our house—a girl named Gobija Zaksauskas—turned out to be an assassin with a hit list of names. With Gobi's gun to my head, we'd spent the night careening around New York City in my father's Jaguar while she killed her targets one by one, ending with my house getting blown up. Describing the night as "insane" could arguably be considered an insult to the mentally ill.

"Your family was all right?"

"Yes."

"And they never found that woman's body?"

"Destroyed in the fire," I said. "That's what they think, anyway."

"Wow." We stood there for a moment, and she seemed to realize that she hadn't introduced herself. "I'm Paula Daniels."

She held out her hand, and I shook it in that smiling, somewhat awkward way that people shake hands when they're flirting, and it occurred to me that that's what we were doing. When a couple of people stepped past us on their way through the door, Paula edged a little closer, her bare shoulder brushing against my arm, and the party noise seemed to fade way down in the mix so it was as if just the two of us were standing there talking to each other. Something happened right then. It was that weightless moment when you stop worrying about riding the bike and just starting riding it.

"Can I ask you a personal question?" she said.

"Sure."

"Was it all true?"

"Are you kidding?" I said. "I couldn't have made that stuff up."

"I had a feeling." A tiny smile touched the corner of her lips and echoed in her eyes with a shimmer that I could almost hear, like the soft chime of an incoming text message. "I pride myself on my ability to separate truth and bullshit."

"That's a rare talent," I said.

"Not as marketable as it used to be."

"Maybe you should be a detective."

She laughed an easy, natural laugh. "I bet you get asked that a lot."

"What?"

"You know—fact or fiction."

"Actually, no," I said. "It's weird, but most people don't really seem to care."

And it was true. They had read about what happened with me and Gobi on prom night in New York in the newspapers and seen it on TV, posted about it on their blogs, forwarded it and "liked" it on Facebook and tweeted about it to their friends. As far as the American public was concerned, what happened to us that night

203

was the truth, yet another improbable chunk of "reality" gone viral in a post-MTV world, and everybody had just kind of accepted it and moved on.

"So you're not a detective," I said.

"No."

"What do you do besides read the Post and go to parties in Brooklyn?"

She smiled, cocked an eyebrow. "There's more to life?"

"Depends who you ask, I guess."

"Fair enough. The truth is, I work in the music industry."

I felt my heart do a little stumble-step in my chest, because this conversation really did seem to be entering the department of Too Good to Be True. "Really."

"Yes."

"You know," I said, "that's funny, because I sort of play in a band."

"Inchworm." Paula nodded. "I remember from the story."

"Yeah." I was starting to think I could really fall in love with this girl. "Well, ah, anyway . . . we all decided to take a year off before college, just to see if we can make something happen. If not . . ." I shrugged.

"If you don't try, you'll always wonder."

I nodded. "Exactly."

"You should slip me your demo."

"Seriously?"

"Absolutely. I work for this European promoter, George Armitage—"

"Wait a second," I said. "*The* George Armitage?"

"That's him."

"Are you kidding? Armitage is, like, the hottest promoter in the world right now. Ever since the Enigma festival in the U.K. last summer, plus he owns his own airline . . . You actually work for that guy?"

Paula smiled. "Well, I'm sort of the liaison between him and the labels. Technically I'm on Armitage's payroll, but I spend about half my time in L.A., working with new bands in the studio. It's kind of a position that I created for myself."

"That sounds amazing."

"I grew up in Laurel Canyon." Paula reached up, tucked a strand of hair behind her ear. "My father was an A&R guy back in the day, worked with all the legends—Fleetwood Mac, Steely Dan, the Eagles. Madonna and Sean Penn practically got a divorce in our pool. It's in my blood."

And that was how it started. People talk about fate and luck and blind chance, and even now I'm not sure where I stand on those issues, but I will say this: In the weeks and months that Paula and I got more serious, I found her to be exactly as confident, ambitious, imaginative, and funny as she was that first night, and as I got to know her better, I sort of ran out of adjectives. She was that mixed mouthful of flavors, the kind of person that would walk through a farmer's market and in the middle of a conversation about Soviet cinema in the 1940s, pick up two bananas and pretend they were her eyebrows.

And she was unfathomably beautiful, totally out of my league. The kind of girl you write songs about. She was twenty-two years old, and I was eighteen.

Then again, historically, I tend to prefer older women.